Leabharlann Chontae Uíbh Fhailí

offaly c

D0783643

a year of our lives

JOHN MacKENNA

a year of our lives

PICADOR

First published 1995 by Picador

an imprint of Macmillan General Books
Cavaye Place London SW10 9PG
and Basingstoke

Associated companies throughout the world

ISBN 0 330 33956 7

Copyright © John MacKenna 1995

The right of John MacKenna to be identified as the
author of this work has been asserted by him in accordance
with the Copyright, Designs and Patents Act 1988.

In 'Absent Child' the lyrics from 'Ballad of the Absent Mare',
by Leonard Cohen, publisher Carlin/Quartet,
from the 1979 Columbia album
Recent Songs, are used by permission.

All rights reserved. No reproduction, copy or transmission
of this publication may be made without written permission.
No paragraph of this publication may be reproduced, copied
or transmitted save with written permission or in accordance
with the provisions of the Copyright Act 1956 (as amended).
Any person who does any unauthorised act in relation to
this publication may be liable to criminal prosecution
and civil claims for damages.

1 3 5 7 9 8 6 4 2

A CIP catalogue record for this book is available from
the British Library

Typeset by CentraCet Limited, Cambridge
Printed by Mackays of Chatham, Kent

Leabharlann
Chontae Uíbh Fhailí

Cl.____ F
Ac. 95/678

95/256

Stg£9.99 IR£10.30

for jarlath and clare mackenna

contents

contents

the things we say

It wasn't my idea to come back here on our honeymoon. I'd have chosen somewhere that wasn't home but my husband was so enthusiastic about the prospect of spending time in the place where I was born and grew up that I finally agreed and, anyway, it wasn't as if we needed privacy or anything like that. It was a holiday, I suppose, as much as a honeymoon.

Not that it all began auspiciously. Among the people on the bus that took us the last sixty miles to my village was Robert Holland. He didn't speak but he stared at me so that my husband noticed.

'Do you know that man?' he asked.

'Vaguely,' I said. 'He came on holidays to the village when I was a kid.'

'He must have been impressed. He hasn't taken his eyes off you.'

I laughed it off and hoped nothing more would come of it.

How long since I last saw him? Five or six years? Not

that there was anything sinister in seeing him, just an ominous feeling that may turn out to be completely unfounded. There was nothing worth mentioning to my husband, nothing that I could explain, nothing that would make any sense in the cold light of day. It was all wrapped up inside me, still is, maybe always will be.

And then the bus was clattering into the village and my mother was on the Square. My brother was cycling down the hill, late as usual, and taking the bags on his bicycle.

Walking to the house, we heard two cuckoos calling from the fields near the cliffs.

'That's for good luck,' my husband said.

'Is it?'

'Of course it is. It has to be.'

Immediately I regretted my curtness.

'Yes, good luck and good fortune,' my mother said.

The wiser woman.

My brother was at the house before us, the bags upstairs, glasses and a bottle of wine on the kitchen table. My mother looked over the photographs from the Registry Office, hiding her disappointment. My brother toasted our good sense in keeping things simple and inexpensive. My husband talked about the two cuckoos again. My brother said they were devious birds, untrustworthy. My brother who is so like me.

'I saw Robert Holland getting off the bus,' he said, once the birds had been dismissed.

'Yeah.'

'He wasn't here at all last summer. He must be back to do something on the house. It needs painting.'

I nodded.

'Do I know him?' my husband asked.

'The guy on the bus,' I said.

'Another broken heart she left behind,' my brother said.

'Not true,' I said, laughing. 'And now we're going out for some sunshine. Tomorrow it could be raining.'

We walked through the village, out on to the coast road, past the Martello tower and on to the sleeping-ground hill. The sleeping-ground runs down the back of the hill. Green mounds and grey stones that finally melt into the dunes at the beach.

I took my husband into the sleeping-ground and showed him my father's grave. And then we walked down to the dunes, passing Mrs Holland's grave. But I said nothing. We waded through the heavy sand on the dunes and then back up the hill, climbing into the fields and walking along the clifftop and into the lanes that twist back into the village. While we were walking, the sky changed. It sucked up the spray from the cliffs, turned the white water grey and spat it out again. We sheltered under a wall blackened with rain, hunkering on the grass.

As the rain grew harder we crouched lower and then my husband lay back and pulled me down on top of him, opening my shirt and sucking my breasts, pushing my jeans down until his fingers were inside me, until I wanted him inside me, until I'd opened his jeans and I was fucking him. Until we both came, his hands showering me with flowers and blades of grass and clay, his face flecked with rain and sweat. We lay there for a long time afterwards, letting the rain puddle on our skin. We might have been discovered but that didn't worry me.

'You're my saviour,' my husband said.

I smiled at him. 'How?'

'Every time we fuck in a place like this, somewhere that we don't expect it, it brings me to the edge of madness and then you bring me back again. When I come in you, I'm saved from something I don't understand, something that seems to be waiting for me. I just know I am.'

I smiled at him again.

Sometimes he says things like that. And sometimes they stop me up short and sometimes, like today, my mind is somewhere else and they just about reach me.

And then, tonight, when I came up to our bedroom, my old room, after my mother and brother had gone to bed, my husband had lit candles. On the windowsill and the bedside table and the washstand. We sat on the bed and he ran the backs of his hands up and down my face, very slowly. I like it when he does that.

'Save me again,' he said. 'Be my saviour again.'

He kept saying that while we fucked again and I tried to be quiet when I came, biting into his skin, biting as deep and as hard as I dared.

And then we both fell asleep. I must have woken after ten or fifteen minutes. The candles were still burning and my husband was lying with his arms thrown across the bed.

My crucified saviour, I thought, and I smiled.

I was ten the first time the Hollands came to the village. I shared this room with my sister then and we had a candle for light. I'd see the Hollands in the village. Mrs Holland was elegant and slim and dark. Her husband was grey-haired and tanned but his tan was different from the burned skin of the fishermen whose boats lined the quay. His was an even colour. Robert was a child of my own age.

The Hollands bought a house on the other side of the hill. Some weeks I'd see them every day – at the shop or buying fish on the quay – and sometimes I wouldn't see them for days.

'The English,' my brother called them.

When I heard them talking, in the shop, I knew what he meant. Their accents were English, very English. They stood out and, as a result, people either avoided them or were drawn to making them feel at home. We seem always to have been like that in the village. There's no middle ground. In everything there are extremes, no middle ground. Perhaps it's the lives we've lived on the edge of the land and the edge of the sea.

Whenever the chance came, I'd watch Mrs Holland on the quay, dressed in her kaftan. She had confidence and grace that I admired but never achieved myself. She was the kind of woman I'd have gone on admiring had she lived. Sometimes I'd see her on the beach in her swimsuit. She and her husband swam several times a day, strongly along the line of the coast while I kept to my depth, but then I was the only swimmer in our family.

'Sea people never swim,' my brother would say. 'Better to go down quick and be done with it.'

I spied on her when she sunbathed on the rocks. I was enthralled by her long brown legs, her plunging swimsuit that seemed backless, her ease with the elements. She was elegance.

The Hollands came back every summer after that. When I was fourteen I thought they were the most perfect and most beautiful family in the world. That was the summer my father died.

I rarely talk about my father, not because I have no clear memories of him, I do, and not because he wasn't important to me, he was, but because he was always part of whatever certainty there was in our house and I still think of him as that. As whatever quiet certainty there is behind my life, even now.

The Hollands came up to our house the day my father died. They spoke to my mother and brother. They offered the use of their car for the funeral. And Mrs Holland spoke to me. I don't remember what she said, I don't think I heard the words. I was mesmerized by the reassurance of her tone. I felt everything would be all right. She sounded so certain that I couldn't doubt her.

Later that summer my sister went away to stay with my aunt and in the same week the electrical storms began. We always had storms in the summer but these seemed to come every night. I'd lie in the darkness, terrified, and then the light would snap and unsnap, a second of light which unveiled shadows, faces, figures. My father's face? His outline? His hand on the windowsill? I wanted my father to come back and I dreaded his arrival. I wanted to call out to my mother but something stopped me. And then, reacting to my silence, a figure in the doorway. My brother. Holding me in his arms. Shushing me gently. Singing quietly. What was it he sang? I can't remember. Jesus, I can't remember. But he was there when I fell asleep and he was there when I woke, curled in a blanket on the floor beside my bed.

The storms went on. Night after night, into a second week and a third.

'They'll kill us,' I said, one night when the sheet-lightning rose out of the sea and dipped the village in a wash of blue and white.

My brother took me to the window. 'Sit there,' he said. 'Don't move. Count to twenty and don't move. Just keep watching the back field.'

And then he was gone, reappearing at fifteen in the yard below, climbing the stone wall into the small haggard behind the house, parading around there, dressed only in a blanket, while the sky and the land were fused in thunder-flashes. And then he climbed on to the wall and dropped the blanket and stood there, naked, with his fists driven up into the night while the noise and the light poured over him.

I slept soundly that night and every other night of that flashing summer. Most mornings, when I woke, my brother's blanket was curled on my bedroom floor.

And here's my sleeping husband. I'd like to tell him of how my brother saved me from the dark and the light but he'd think my brother was mad.

Anyway. Anyway, time to blow the candles out.

The same small field. The same stone wall. The same windowsill where I sat and counted to twenty. But what was the song? Tomorrow, sometime when the chance comes I'll ask my brother if he remembers. Or maybe not. He'd be embarrassed and he'd deny the whole thing happened and that would destroy so much. He'd dismiss the whole thing in the way I dismissed my husband's talk about the cuckoos being lucky.

Why are we like that? Is it an ocean cynicism? Does it come with the uncertainty of the sea? Or is it just us? Just this house, this family? Is it because we had so little that we pretended we needed nothing?

No. That's not entirely it. I wanted things. When I was eight or nine I wanted to fly. I desperately wanted to rise up over the village and see beyond it. I'd watch the black shadows of the swallows zipping across the back yard and I'd wish my shadow could be that fast. Here and gone. Gone somewhere new and exotic. Or just gone. And there were other things. I wanted my father back with us. I wanted Mrs Holland's elegance. I wanted to slip in and out of places without drawing attention to myself. I wanted to be beautiful. Most of all, I wanted to escape and, at the same time, I never wanted to leave.

But nothing happened. Summer ended and it was time to go back to school. Life went grinding on. Winter storms. Skeletons of boats thrown up on the beach. Spring threatening but never coming and then summer again. The buses running twice a day. Daytrippers. The Hollands arriving. School closing. Walking the quay wall with the other girls. Watching and waiting. The summer withering. The last of the summer buses. The Hollands walking the beach for the last time, swimming their last swim. Tying their cases on to the roofrack of their car, waving goodbye. And then the quay was empty, apart from the trawlers, and it was time for school again.

I was fifteen. Sixteen. Seventeen.

Anyway. Anyway, time to blow the candles out.

I can hear my husband breathing. That makes me wife again. It feels the same as it did and yet there is no comparison. Being married then was much the same as now. And then it changed. And this may change. No matter how good things are they may not be good enough. I learned that and it stalks me now. The better things are the worse they may be when they're gone.

Sometimes I think the black days are our safeguard, the days when there's nothing to do but let him sink until he's ready to come back up without any help, until he's able to do it. I've learned enough to know I can't rescue him. Those may be the times that save me, if I ever need saving. Those may be the memories that will keep me afloat if I'm thrown back on my own. Those are the saving graces, not the days when he's flying, when his happiness is intense. The times when he's inside me, when he's a different person, when he doesn't speak because he's lost in me, are useless afterwards.

That kind of exhilaration comes back to haunt. It's the memory of blackness that helps, that proves life can be better. What would he think, this husband who tells me fucking with me makes him feel like God on the edge of creation? He smiles when I joke about creation but he doesn't really listen. What would he think if he knew I store up the sensations of exclusion because I know I may need them someday? Of course I admire his appetite for passion but I'm grateful for the balance that keeps me in control.

The sky is cloudy but there's a full moon behind the cloud. The yard is more sallow than white but everything is clear, right across the fields and down to the shore. The light isn't brilliant but it has a kind of serenity. Isn't serenity enough? I thought about that on the bus coming out here. My husband asked me a hundred questions about the village, about growing up here, about the people and the places I knew. He was like a child. And then he asked me to take him to the first place I'd ever made love, to take him there and fuck with him.

'Why,' I said. 'It's not jealousy, is it?'

He looked hurt when I said that, as though I hadn't understood. 'Of course not. I just want to be everywhere that's you. Your house. Your room. The place where you first made love. The place where you were born. The place you went to school. That's all.'

'I lived here for eighteen years,' I told him. 'How long have we got?'

He smiled at that. 'Just that once,' he said. 'Just that one place.'

And when we came up to this room, tonight, when he took off my clothes, when we lay down together, I said, 'Here, this is where I first made love.'

'Tell me about it,' he said.

And I told him a story. About a boy who'd followed me around all that summer, my seventeenth. Robert Holland. He'd come for the summer with his parents, as always. But this time it was different. His mother had changed. She was no longer elegant. She was ill and haggard and wasted. She was dying.

Mr Holland went everywhere with her. They walked the beach, slowly. To anyone who didn't know them, they looked like a couple lost in conversation, as indeed they were. But, to those of us who knew, everything had changed. They walked too closely together. They were wrapped up in each other. Her faded body seemed to fold itself into the shadow of her husband. They were holding on to whatever little was left to them and the closer they walked the wider the gulf that was before them. Even then, even as a young girl, I had some notion of that. I might not have understood it completely but I suspected the horror that lay ahead for them. To see that once elegant woman being carried by her husband against the wind told everything.

I stopped watching them. I couldn't bear to see her melting away. I avoided the beach at the times I knew they'd be there. I never walked to the side of the hill their house was built on. I tried to forget what Mrs Holland had been and what she was.

But Robert was watching me, following me. And I was sorry for him. I made a point of talking to him. It was difficult. I'd known him so long and never spoken to him, beyond a word on the road, and now, wherever I went, he was there. Waiting for me to talk. So I did. Not that we ever talked a lot. He was as shy as I was and the silence helped both of us. We both knew how much effort was involved and we both respected the other's fear.

Afterwards, I wondered about that time. About Robert and his parents. Did he feel excluded by his parents or was he terrified of watching his mother's life drip away? He seemed to avoid his parents as much as I did. He hung around our house a lot. My mother fed him. And then it happened. We were here together one afternoon. Alone. I came upstairs to get something and he followed me. I turned around and he was standing in the doorway of my room. It just happened. No great event. He knew less about it than I did. I wasn't leading or being led. It was just something.

'Did you love him?' my husband asked.

'I felt tenderness towards him. I felt sorry for him. I

liked him. He was handsome. He still is, you've seen that.'

And I told my husband about the rest of that summer. About how I went on sleeping with Robert Holland. About how we learned things together, simple things about each other's bodies.

And then his mother died.

'They buried her here in the village, in the sleeping-ground,' I told my husband. 'She was thirty-eight years old.'

I cried, remembering her. Such a beautiful woman and the terrifying sadness she left in her wake. So different from the feelings when my father died. Such a sense of complete waste.

'Everything about her was wasted,' I said. 'Her body, her grace, her possibilities.'

'I'm sorry,' my husband said. 'I shouldn't have asked. It was none of my business. I didn't mean to do this.'

And he rubbed the backs of his hands against my face, very slowly.

'Save me again,' he said. 'Be my saviour again.'

He kept saying that while we fucked.

The things we say, the questions we ask each other, fearing the truth, yet hunting it down to its bitter end. But some of what I told my husband tonight was true and the rest wasn't worth telling. Not because I'm ashamed of it but because he wouldn't understand. Just as Robert Holland didn't. Just as his father didn't – not really. But Mrs Holland would have done, I know she would.

Still, it wasn't all my husband's fault. All this remembering. There was Robert Holland on the bus. Mrs Holland's grave. And the small inscription at the foot of her headstone. The inscription I'd almost forgotten. Let me tell my husband now. While he's sleeping. Then he can hear whatever he needs to hear and the rest can go unremembered.

Mrs Holland was dying. That much is true. Everyone could see it. To see her husband and herself together was to see that. Where once they complemented each other they now, literally, leaned together with an awkwardness I can't describe. People passing, people who knew the situation, were uneasy. We felt as if we were intruding. I think Robert felt that way too. He wanted them to have whatever half-chance remained to remember and relive the past.

Maybe I knew, with the intuition of the young, that he needed someone to get him through that time. And, maybe, I was flattered by the thought that I could be the one. We were there for each other. Maybe it was as simple as that. Sometimes the most clichéd explanations are the truest.

He might have stumbled across someone else and so might I but we didn't. We spent those weeks walking, swimming, kissing, talking when we had to, when there was nothing else to do. Once or twice he came up to my room, when the place was empty, and lay with me on my bed but he seemed to have no energy, no passion, no desire to do anything. We'd lie face to face cocooned in our separateness, everything that his parents weren't. Whatever satisfaction existed stemmed from his sadness and my attempts at comfort. He was concerned with his dying mother and I was concerned with myself. We were only slightly concerned with each other.

And then his mother died, one morning in July.

I went up to their house that afternoon. The curtains were all open. Even the window in the dead room was wide to the breeze from the sea. I'd never seen that before. My father, like everyone else who died in our village, lay in a dark room that was perfectly still. Mrs Holland lay in a room that filled and emptied with the swing of the wind and the stuttering of the sea. The sun streamed across the floor and on to the brass bedstead. Everything was white with light and her body seemed to be nothing more than a flimsy transfer on this cotton sheet. I had to look carefully to be sure she was really there. Her skin seemed to appear and disappear as the wind filled and emptied the room. Was this a body or a ghost? Was this the woman I'd known or a reflection off the sea? One thing I did know – she was no longer beautiful. There was an emptiness in her face. No trace that life had ever been there, no sign of beauty. Nothing of her left.

Mrs Holland was buried in the sleeping-ground the following afternoon. No church, no prayers. Her husband read a poem at the grave.

Years later, I heard someone read the same poem on the radio and discovered it was 'Crossing the Bar'. I went to the library and found it and copied it. I still have it somewhere in a drawer. I know that late that night, the night of Mrs Holland's burial, there was an orange sunset that bled the whole sky out over the sea. And, later still, there was the evening star above the house where the Hollands had lived for so many summers, the house where she had died.

I didn't see Robert in the week after his mother's death. I waited for him in the place we normally went but he didn't come and I didn't dare go up to the house again. I did go to the sleeping-ground most evenings, partly to visit his mother's grave, partly in the hope of seeing him. Even then I thought it strange that I should be drawn to where this woman was buried. I rarely went near my father's grave but somehow there was something about Mrs Holland's youth and beauty that said, Come and look and savour the tragedy. I think I almost needed her, needed to be near her, needed to breathe the dead air and watch the dying flowers on the dry sands. I can't explain this. I was young, I was impressionable and I was lost but those are facts and they don't explain a lot.

But it wasn't evening, it was morning when it happened. A bright blue and yellow morning, just after seven. A morning at the start of August, when summer crams everything into a final thrust of heat and the particular light of summertime. I'd woken very early and couldn't sleep again, so I went swimming and now I was making for home, crossing the sleeping-ground. And then I saw Mr Holland. He was standing in a dip in the ground, about fifty yards from his wife's grave, not even looking at it. Instead, he was watching me. I stopped when I saw him, the red towel I was carrying trailing in the seagrass that keeps the graves anchored to this earth.

'Don't stand so far away from me,' Mr Holland said.

I moved towards him but very slowly. I was a little frightened.

'Stand here,' he said, pointing.

I went and stood beside him.

He was silent.

I could barely hear his breathing. Short, soft breaths. I wanted him to speak, to say something that would break this terrible silence. I wished someone would come and disturb us but I knew the beach behind me was empty.

He stood there, staring out past me, across the waves of sharp grass, breathing those soft breaths. I thought he was going to die. And then, suddenly, he had my hand in his but nothing was said. I waited for him to do something. I expected him to scream or to cry but he didn't. Nothing. Breathing. The sea away behind me. The sand beginning to dazzle as the sun moved higher.

'Are you all right?'

I heard my own voice and was surprised by its strength and calmness. He turned, only slightly, so that his face was close to mine. I expected his eyes to be filled with tears, but they weren't. I thought he might kiss me but, again, I was wrong. Instead, he stared at me and then knelt down slowly and let go of my hand.

'Let me see you,' he said, in a whisper. 'Please, let me see you.'

I dropped the towel I was holding and undid the buttons on the front of the light dress I was wearing over my swimsuit. I rolled the dress off my shoulder and it fell, loosely, down my arms, only catching at my waist.

'Let me see you,' he said again.

I pulled the straps of the swimsuit off my shoulders, first one and then the other. I stopped for an instant but only an instant and then I peeled the damp swimsuit from my breasts and stood there, facing him.

'You're very beautiful,' he said.

'Am I?' My voice, but I couldn't believe I was speaking.

'Am I?' I asked again.

'Very.'

I took his head in my hands and pressed his face against my belly. I felt the unshaven skin against my skin. My fingers were tight in his hair.

'You smell of life,' he said, the words coming up, muffled by my belly. 'No, you smell of sea. You smell of salt water.'

I held him to me a little while longer and then relaxed my hands. The wind was blowing against my skin, lighter and cooler than it had been. I thought of two things. I thought of rain. I wished it would rain, I wanted it to rain on me. I had almost forgotten that Mr Holland was still there. I wanted to feel rain on my skin, I wanted to sense rain running off my shoulder, making streams on my body. And then I thought of possibility – the possibility of my life. For the first time, maybe the only time, in my life

I felt that I was in charge of everything that would happen to me. I was mistress of my destiny.

Mr Holland had eased himself away from me. He was sitting back on his hunkers, his eyes on the ground. I think he had forgotten me, too. I pulled my dress back over my shoulders and buttoned it. The cotton felt strange against my breasts but I left my swimsuit about my waist. I did all this very slowly and then I picked my towel from the sand and walked away.

I didn't feel power over him. I didn't feel remorse. I felt released from childhood and, despite everything, I've never regretted what happened that morning. I've never seen anything wrong in it. For either of us. What was I to him? An angel of life, an attempt at reaffirmation? Perhaps. But my wings were too light to carry him out of that place and state. My wings were new. If I could have saved him I would but I didn't know how. I wasn't even aware that he needed saving. But I can't blame myself for that.

It was the evening of that day when Robert Holland came to our house. My mother and brother had just gone out. I think he must have watched and waited until I was alone. I was sitting in the kitchen, reading, in the dusky light and he walked in, without knocking, and stood at the table.

I put down my book and stood up but before I could speak he took me by the hand and led me upstairs to my room. He undid my buttons and let my dress fall to the floor. He kissed my belly and eased me on to my bed, kneeling beside me and easing his hand inside my pants, beginning to slide his fingers inside me. I closed my eyes and let him go on masturbating me. I didn't want him to stop and I was already too far gone to do anything for him. I just wanted his fingers inside me, I wanted him to go on stroking me. I wanted to come. Then I'd do whatever he wanted. Then. But for now it was me.

Suddenly his fingers stopped. My first thought was that my mother or my brother had come into the room. I opened my eyes. We were alone but Robert was standing up, glowering.

'I saw you,' he said. 'I saw what you did.'

He started to cry.

'Don't,' I said. 'Lie down with me.'

He spat on me and walked out of my room. He went so quietly that, for a while, I thought he was outside my door, but he was gone.

I saw him again during the rest of that summer. Of course I did. I saw him the next night and the next and every night for the next two weeks. I saw him coming in on one of the trawlers in the twilight. I saw him talking with the fishermen and the police. I saw him walking to his house where he had stayed every night since his father went missing. My mother had sent my brother up to invite him to stay with us. He thanked her but said he was all right where he was. I never saw him during the day. He was out on the boats, searching. My brother said the body would turn up in ten or twelve days but it didn't. It never appeared. Nor did Robert the following summer. The house stayed locked and shuttered.

After that he came back only at odd intervals and when he did he always spent the first few days walking the beach and the rocks, searching, it seemed to us. As if he didn't believe we had kept watch all that first winter. As if the trawlermen didn't check their nets carefully.

But his father's body never appeared and then it went beyond the time when it might.

'For such a strong swimmer to do that,' my brother said once.

'Maybe he cut his wrists,' my mother suggested.

'No,' my brother said. 'I've seen that done. He wouldn't have got out far if that was the case. He'd have been washed in before the week was over.'

I left the village that autumn, husband. I began the journey that took me to you. Eventually.

Three summers afterwards, when I was back here with the man who was to be my other husband, I saw the stone on Mrs Holland's grave. 'In loving memory', and all the rest. Name. Dates. And, on the base of the stone, her husband's name and one line: 'May he find peace'.

'There's a life out here that I've never seen anywhere else,' you said to me last night, when we were walking. 'It must be the sea and the wind and the openness to the world across the ocean. This whole world.' But the sea has nothing to do with life, I thought. But I didn't say that. I'd said enough already.

'You smell of life,' he said. 'No, you smell of the sea.'
May he find peace.
May all of us.
And love.

in the garden

Isn't it strange, my dear wife, how you, who accused me of allowing my fascination with the past to become an obsession, are now my obsession. Because you are past, you'd tell me. But that is too trite an assertion. David arrived yesterday, unannounced, to stay with me for the Easter holiday. A year on, he said, to the week. I must need some company.

There, you're saying, the past again. An anniversary. That is the reason for my fascination. But that isn't so, either. All of this is by the way. Let me explain. And, before I do, let me say that all through the winter, when this dream cottage of mine was damp, when I sat here at night thinking that if I fell down dead no one would find me for a week, all through that winter of freedom my only concern was the here and now. I did not go running back to the past.

Let me explain.

I have spent the last five days digging the big wild garden outside. Dragging more than digging. Dragging bindweed out of the earth, pulling the tines of the fork through the sinewy weeds until my fingers blistered and the blisters bled. Six hours the first day, six hours the second, five hours the third. And at the end of the day everthing I had pulled and gathered went up in a twenty second blaze and I was left with a cigarette pile in the corner and a roughly dug patch that mocked the idea of a day's work. And fifteen feet of grass and weed untouched between me and the fence. On every side. And then yesterday I looked up and there was David, leaning over the gate, watching me dig and telling me that kind of thing was lethal for a man in his forties.

'You need to work yourself into that kind of thing,' he grinned. 'When was the last time you dug a garden? When you were first married?'

'Fuck off,' I said.

'Exactly my point. This kind of thing is neither good for the body or the mind. You're stressed!'

Unannounced. Uninvited. And I was bloody glad to see him. Last night we went out for a drink and when we got back he went on drinking in the bare yellow kitchen.

'Easter never made it,' he said.

He gave me no time to answer.

'Easter is where the human and divine parted,' he said. 'Christmas, now that is a human time. Happy ever after. Presents. Little baby. Choirs of scrubbed children. Love. All very well. But Easter is beyond us. Even the early Christians let it go. It floated away from them like a balloon that's slipped its string. Death. Pain. Suffering. Too depressing.'

'There's the resurrection,' I said.

He shook his head, smiled that big deep smile. You know that smile.

'Too much of a leap of faith. Anyway, it's too little, too late. Torture, death, humiliation. Too much to recover from. Not in two days and then the balloon was gone. Up, up and away.'

He turned his hand over, the way he does. I said nothing.

'I'm probably depressing you.'

I shook my head.

'No, I am.' He was insistent. 'And I didn't come here to do that. I'll tell you what — tomorrow we will attack that garden and beat the shit out of the bindweed.'

He swung an imaginary spade over his shoulder, marched to the back door and flicked on the outside light. He stood looking through the glass.

'No problem. We'll come at it from two sides. Phwup. Done.'

'Right,' I said. 'Weapon parade at nine a.m.'

He came back and sat down at the fire. 'Do you remember the Easter your mother and father were in England and I came and stayed at your house. Speaking of parading weapons.'

Note, I was not the one who began this conversation but, yes, I did respond.

'Sligo,' I said.

'Wherever. You were studying and I'd met that girl.

25

Carol. Jesus, what was her second name? Carol something. She worked in a jewellers in Carlow. She came and stayed and stayed and came.' He laughed at his own joke. 'Do you remember her? Huge knockers, short skirts, high boots and always a red blouse. Didn't she always wear red blouses? Or did I imagine that?'

'She did,' I said. 'Short skirts, red blouses.'

'Best blow-job I ever got and she was only nineteen. Why don't we ever marry these women? You tell me that.' His mouth hung open. He shook his head and sprang to his feet and stood there glowering. 'And here we are, forty years old, facing a day pulling bindweed, fucking bindweed out of a garden. Ah, bollocks.'

I tell you all of this because it may amuse you. You may sit there smiling and thinking, He hasn't changed, still the same David. Or you may dismiss it. You may sit there thinking, I haven't changed. Still as infantile. It doesn't really matter, of course. Not now. But I am determined to go on with this because there is a point worth making.

After David had gone to bed I took out my Bible and read that passage I always read on Holy Thursday. I always read it to you. The one that begins:

'He went forth with his disciples over the brook, Cedron, where there was a garden, into the which he entered and his disciples. And Judas also which betrayed him knew the place.'

26

I thought you'd like that. The element of betrayal. Last year I read that passage at our table but we knew what was coming, if not how fast. It may have been like that for Jesus, huddled there among the unreliables, not knowing how quickly the pillars would collapse, not suspecting how painful it all would be. It wasn't always like this, was it? Childhood Easters were full of starched daffodils and crocuses in the sleet. One Easter I was recovering from a long illness and on Good Friday I walked across the fields and smelt the dung from the gardens and I felt good. Life was starting again. But that is the past, isn't? Let me stick with last night.

I closed my Bible and I started humming that hymn you always hummed.

> 'All in the April evening, April airs were abroad,
> the sheep with their little lambs passed me by on the
> road . . .'

You were surprised, the first time you hummed it, that I knew the words. I never told you where they came from but I will now. It's all part of proving a point. Last night, sitting in the yellow kitchen, it struck me that out there, just across the fence, there were sheep and lambs and I felt good. And out there, in the shelter of the shed, there were four dishevelled daffodils. And I walked out across the roughly dug soil and leaned over the fence and listened to the gentle night-time sounds from the end of the field. And I looked at those four daffodils, standing in the light from the kitchen window, and I thought if my father saw them he would turn in his grave. He who had been so proud of his garden, who had been so certain that his drills were straight, who had edged the lawns to a line. He who had sown so many daffodils that they tolled in the dark breezes along the garden path. How often had I listened to their gentle swishing from my bed?

You see, I hear you saying, obsession. Perhaps, if we had been obsessed with each other, this would never have happened. Or perhaps leaving had become the obsession. Gentle memory always slid into obsession, you said, and perhaps you were right. It isn't that I haven't carried guilt but the guilt has never been heavy enough to do anything more than slow me down. And partly it is because the past is a safe place. Safe in its distance and its loss. You said that once. You told me I was obsessed with all the people I had lost. Well, let me tell you one more story now. One well-kept secret. I stood in that bloody garden, last night, and thought of this. Of that Easter when David stayed and Carol stayed. Let me tell you one more story. A story that leaked back into my memory despite myself.

That was the Easter when I met Ellen Burgess, the rector's daughter. Of course, I already knew her. There wasn't anyone I didn't know in our village but I had never spoken to her before. We met at a dance in Carlow. She was drunk and I was bored. We sat in the bar of the dance-hall and she talked, incessantly. About her father, who frowned on drinking, she said; about her mother, who was in John of God's, drying out; about school and life behind the rectory walls – she hated both in equal measure.

She took a lift home with us. She sat in the back with me. David and Carol sat in the front. I remember how ruthlessly she discouraged David's attempts at humour. He dropped us on the Square and drove on up to my house, where he and Carol had taken over my parents' bedroom. I walked Ellen to the rectory gate.

'My father is in there,' she told me, pointing through the trees, 'sleeping the sleep of the just and self-satisfied. And my mother is sleeping elsewhere. She's bloated and baggy now. When I was a kid she was the most beautiful woman I'd ever seen. He wrecked her. He doesn't even see that.'

'I don't think you should be telling me this,' I said.

'Why not?' she asked. She jumped up and down, tearing a branch from a laburnum that hung out over the rectory wall and twirling it in my face. 'How long have you lived here?'

'All my life,' I said.

'I've been here since I was seven. Ten years. I've never spoken to you before. Time to make up. Anyway he is an arrogant bastard. I don't care who knows. And now I'll stop talking.' She slid her hands inside my open coat and pulled me towards her. Leaning back against the wall, she pulled me closer and then she kissed me, sliding her tongue into my mouth. It tasted of whiskey. The kiss went on a long time and then she pushed my head away. 'And how many times more will we talk?'

'As often as you like,' I said.

She smiled a sly smile. 'Don't you believe it.'

'I'd like to see you again,' I said.

'I bet you would. Protestant girls do it, is that what you've heard?'

I said nothing.

'I'll come and call on you tomorrow afternoon,' she said. 'My father will be away for a couple of hours. He might not approve. Purely on biological grounds. Will you be there?'

'Yes,' I said. 'I'll be studying.'

She kissed me again but this time quickly and then she was gone. I picked the broken, budding branch from the path and walked home. I put the branch in a glass and put it in my bedroom window. I tried not to listen to David and Carol in the room next door. And then I fell asleep and probably dreamed. Of a great seduction. But, in the end, it was she who seduced me.

She came and called the following afternoon and we walked down the river, past Joe Shea's bridge, across the Rocks, back by the Mill Pond and in by the Barrack Road.

You see, I've forgotten very little. Par for the course, you'll say. Standing in the garden, in the darkness I imagined I could pick out the light of the rectory last night. Four miles away across the fields now. Of course I was mistaken. But yes, we walked back arm in arm and we lay on my bed and I kissed her mouth and her tongue tasted strangely different. I remember that. And afterwards David came back and she was as dismissive as she had been the night before. And when she was leaving I asked if I could see her the following day. Holy Thursday.

'Wait for me in the churchyard. I have damn choir practice,' she said. 'I'll get away as early as I can. It won't be for long but I'll get away.'

I waited in the churchyard. It was a dry hot day and the sunshine split through the branches and splintered over the flat and crooked stones. I lay on one, watching the crows circling and soaring in and out of the opening in the bell-tower beside the church. The organ churned, the voices rang through the empty church, the words came cleanly across the newly mown grass, like scent in themselves.

'All in the April evening, April airs were abroad,
the sheep with their little lambs passed me by on the road.
Up in the blue, blue mountains, pastures are sweet,
rest for the little bodies, rest for the little feet.'

Such a desperately sad song. And the voices went on singing:

'I saw the sheep with their little lambs and thought on the
    lamb of God.'

The music swirled and died. Voices through the open window. A shadow across my face. And there she was.

'I only have a few minutes,' she said.

'What about tomorrow?'

'Tomorrow is bad. I'm expected here for service. Saturday night is good. My father will be away. All night. You come down to the house. I'll be on my own. And I don't really want to have to spend the night with the other pair. I'll telephone you.'

And before I could sit up she was gone again, weaving through the tipsy stones. The organ moaned another tune. I lay back in the sunshine. Frightened. Exhilarated.

Am I doing justice to your expectations? Have I remembered sufficient detail? I know I've been weak on the senses but maybe that will be clarified by the rest of what I have to tell you. Don't be over critical. Not yet.

She did telephone on the Saturday evening, just after seven. I walked across the land drainage yard, cutting between the diggers and caterpillar tractors to the back of the rectory. She saw me scrambling through the garden and waved from the dining-room window.

We sat in that room and drank coffee. I admired a photograph of her parents.

'Do you know what he preached on yesterday?' she asked.

I shook my head.

'On the mote in your brother's eye and the beam in your own. I've heard him return to that so often. And he never sees the point of it, he never sees the bloody great log that's across our family, never. I keep waiting for him to make the connection.'

I thought she was going to cry, with anger or sadness. I asked if she was all right.

She smiled a blazing smile. 'You'll get used to me. I'm just glad you're here to talk to.' She held out her hand and

I crossed to where she was sitting and knelt in front of her chair. She held my head in her hands and then pressed my face against her breasts. The sweet smell of her body and her clothes. 'I can be very gentle and very loving, you'll see,' she said. 'But I hate him so much.'

I wanted her to stop talking about her father. I pulled my face away and knelt up and kissed her.

'Just forget him for a while,' I said.

She went on smiling. 'This is silly,' she said, taking my hands and pulling me up with her. 'Let's go to bed.'

She led me up two flights of stairs. It was dark but she didn't turn on a light until we reached her bedroom. It was a dim bedside lamp. Immediately, she began to take off her clothes. She noticed my hesitation. 'Don't,' she said. 'Please don't.'

Something wakened me a long time later. I looked at my watch. It was twenty past one. A light shone from the landing across her bed. She was awake.

'Did I hear something?'

'Just a car.'

'Why is the landing light on?'

'Just for comfort,' she said. 'Go back to sleep.'

Suddenly there were steps on the stair.

'Jesus,' I froze.

The footsteps passed the half-open door of Ellen's room.

'Is that you, daddy?' she called.

The sound of the footsteps came back along the landing and the door was pushed open. The light starched everything. She sat up, her breasts uncovered as she turned to me and kissed me lightly on the head. I saw her father's face, the skin loose and haggard, in the instant before he turned away. I'm sure he never focused on my face. I was just a figure. And then the footsteps went heavily down the stairs.

Ellen said nothing. Stepping from the bed, she pulled on a dressing gown and followed him. I stumbled after her, cursing my clothes and shoes. By the time I'd dressed they were both downstairs. I followed, tentatively. She was leaning against the jamb of the dining room door. I stopped behind her, feeling I must say something but there was nothing to say. Her father was slumped in the armchair I'd sat in earlier. She was smiling at him. And then she became aware of my presence.

'You can go,' she said.

And I did. Scampering across their garden and into the street. Joining the stragglers going home from midnight Mass. In confusion. In pain.

It wasn't the events that came to me last night, out there, more the sense of pain again, the loss of self respect. I just stood there and felt that cold feeling again. I wanted it to go away, I wanted no part of that memory but there was nothing I could do to exorcize it. And then David broke the spell. I had assumed he was asleep but there he was, stumbling across the heavy sods.

'Are you all right?'

'I'm fine,' I said.

'What were you doing out here?'

'I was thinking,' I said.

'What the hell about?'

'About the night that's in it,' I half lied. 'About Geth-semane, that stuff. It sort of came alive out here.'

'About frigging betrayal,' he said. 'You didn't betray anyone. Neither of you did. It just happened. You got to a stage, it was time to go. That's all. Wasn't it you told me one time that marriage was invented for people who married at fourteen and died at twenty-six. You've done your time. Both of you. Let it go.'

'You're right,' I said.

'Now,' he said. 'I'm going back inside. I'm making tea. I'm not going to sleep at all. Crack of dawn I'll be out here digging. I'm going to dig the shit out of this place. We'll make a garden your father would have been proud of. Right?'

'Right,' I said.

He's sleeping now, my dear wife, in the armchair at the fire. It'll be dawn in a couple of minutes and I'll wake him then. But first I want you to know that not every memory is obsessive and not every obsession is an escape. Not everything comes at my bidding and not every escape is to happiness. It's the loss that takes the longest, the real loss, the real hurt, to leak back through the years but when it comes, like this, it comes to stay.

It's raining out there now but we'll go out and we'll dig and some time around nine or ten we'll start fooling around and one of us will push the other and we'll roll around in the mud like two kids and then we'll come inside and leave the job for the day. We'll shower and make something to eat and doze in the afternoon. And then the sun will come out and we'll talk about what we'll get done tomorrow.

Oh, and just one other thing. It won't get better. I just thought I'd warn you.

the first epistle

Where to begin and how to begin without sending you into a paroxysm of fear that the past has come back like a disease. Perhaps you see it as a disease, appropriate for the age, though they tell us it has changed its pattern of late. It may have taken you a moment to realize what I was getting at, when I first wrote, but then you knew and you know now.

While I sit here in the train, a man on a journey through the snow, you are preparing to make your own journey to meet me. Those are the facts. Two people are preparing to meet. I don't know the details of your preparation. I can only tell you what I am doing now. If I am forced to examine my circumstances in detail then I need to rearrange what I have already written.

I am a grey, forty-three-year-old man, sitting comfortably in a train, writing. I am a Catholic priest. You wouldn't necessarily know that by looking at me, though some people maintain there's something about clerics that shines through any disguise. My disguise is a casual jacket,

37

shirt, sweater, corduroy trousers. Do the dark socks give it away? Hardly, not that shade of blue – dark but distinctly blue. And if the cleric shines through, what do the couple opposite make of me? Do they assume I am writing a sermon, are they impressed that the book left casually on the table is an H. E. Bates or does that simply date me? *The Song of the Wren*, never heard of it, is that what they're thinking? Can't be any bloody good, too thin, is that what they're thinking?

So, I'm a priest. So? Fine.

Being on a train, when I might have driven, might signify something. I chose this means of travel. I need time to relax, to prepare myself, to write this letter to you. Eight weeks ago I made this same journey by car. Out of Dublin on a dirty wet Friday afternoon. Midland towns, snappy drivers, twisting home. Then I was travelling to bury your wife.

You had stood in the hospital mortuary while I led the prayers. You were in the car in front of me as we drove to the church. I stayed in the local hotel, concelebrated the funeral Mass with the local curate, read the prayers at the graveside, had lunch with the closest friends and relatives and then drove back to Dublin.

I checked, by phone, that weekend that you were getting through it all. And that afternoon, after I'd spoken to you, I began to write that letter in my head. It was a cold, dry afternoon and I was walking through Grafton Street and I began to devise what I could say. That night, I put it tentatively on paper. I rewrote it again and again. When the final draft was done, I realized it was on presbytery paper. It looked all wrong. So I wrote it again and this time it seemed to come out right. I sent it with your Christmas card. There was a point in that. If you found it all too much there was the way out of your dilemma.

'What card, what letter? The post is crazy at this time of the year, isn't it?' you could say.

But that was all a different time, not long ago but a different time. I could hardly face the thought of driving down this afternoon. How are you facing the drive to meet me? You should be leaving about now. You'll be there on time, sitting in the warm car, music on the radio, light classical, the engine idling, the snow plupping on the windscreen, the wiper occasionally clearing it easily. And then, as the train pulls in, you'll walk quickly on to the top platform, wait till you see me emerge from a carriage, and come down the steps, hand out, smiling. As so often in the past.

Never in the snow but otherwise as so often in the past.

We are both journeying now. You from your farm where the stock is well cared for. Me from my parish – my parish, my fax, my phone, my parish secretary who rubber stamps so much of what I do. I've left her the car while I'm away. That and the photocopier and a thousand things to do, the same as any week. I need never see a parishioner, there's enough to do without ever hearing a confession, baptizing a child, marrying a smiling couple, burying the dead. But I do those things, too.

But you know all that, we've talked about the humbug often enough. The humbug and the collar.

And if all this is wrong, is so far wide of the mark that you are laughing about it to yourself, then I'll go back to the machinery of parish life. Being a good priest. That is the mundane drug of my survival.

When you got my letter in the Christmas post, you rang me right away. 'Are you all right, has anything happened?' you said.

You were straight enough to call me, I had to be straight enough not to hide behind pretence. 'Everything is fine,' I said.

I was careful, in the final draft of that letter, to tell you exactly what I wanted to tell you. Whatever ghosts were emerging I wanted them to be the ghosts we both knew well. I was careful to say everything. Everything. Right back to your father's farm. My father always sang your father's praises because the farm was well stocked, well cared for. 'That man loves the land,' he'd say. 'You can tell by looking.'

And he was right. Everything had a place and everything was cared for. No torn sacks on the headlands, no rusty gates, no car doors stuck in ditches. And trees left growing along the ditches, cared for.

I'd say all this to your face. If you want to hear me say, watch me say it, then I will. Just say the word.

And the days of those two summers. Tennis on the court across the yard. Stroke for stroke it went. Some days you, some days me. Lost in the game if we knew your mother was about. But when she left to shop we'd be inside before the car had reached the gate. Inside and up that wide, worn stairs, your hand pulling me down on to the bed. Your arms about me, your hands behind my head, hugging me to you. How many days of hugging before I had the courage to kiss you?

On wet days we'd mope about the house until your mother threw us out. As if that was some kind of absolution. And away across the fields, our boots throwing sprays of muck across the drills, down into Lynch's wood. Struggling into the low dry spot under the blackthorn. A most secluded spot. Away from the rain and the world. Lying back, our faces to the grey world above the dense and thorny branches. And then your hand along my face, your tongue along my neck, your hand along my belly, worked under the loose belt on my trousers, me rolling away at the last second, to keep from coming. I stored up all your letters, postcards from the seaside, photographs of us at school, in tennis gear. Everything. Until the last minute. The last Sunday afternoon before I took the plunge. Made a high fire in my room and burnt them one by one, examining each before it went into the flames. And then I went to take my final vows.

And you? Were you happy to take your wedding vows? Were you satisfied with your share of the kingdom and the glory? A beautiful wife, your father's farm, the willingness to keep it well, a decent life.

Did you roll away from her on nights, as I did from you in the wood? You're right, it isn't my concern. Did those afternoons of ours ever come between you?

Well, for now my life is on hold, left in the care of my

able secretary. Was I being hopeful or foolish in taking a week off? The first of many? The last of all?

Is there any trace of the passion we had in your life? Is it there like a faded paper transfer on the back of a child's hand? It has to be, surely it has to be. Will you take me up that wide, worn stairs again? I want you to. It was me that rolled away and God knows why.

'We have to talk this through,' you said when you telephoned last week. We do.

a year of our lives

xi

She is walking through the woods with the children. They know these woods so well. The children chase and gallop ahead, sliding on the hardened frosty grass where the sun makes no impression. She walks slowly, her hands driven deep in her pockets. She walks steadily. The children pause at the end of the pathway and look back at her, she motions them on – up the hill to the summit. They trot away, their voices slipping sporadically through the trees. She reaches the end of the path and turns to follow them. And then she sees it. A thin blue rope sagging from the heavy branch of a sycamore. It dangles three feet above the ground, its end tied in a thick knot. It has probably been there all summer. Small children have clung desperately to the knot, older ones have sailed effortlessly across the path, wrapping their legs around the rope, calling for someone to push them.

She shivers but she isn't cold. This is barely controlled

shaking. Walk on, she thinks, keep walking, follow the children. But there is no escape from the rope, it becomes another rope, one she has never seen, one that haunted her teenage years. It becomes the rope that Mary Noonan spoke of, the story that Mary Noonan whispered in the midnight dormitory, the horror that Mary Noonan never told to any other girl in the school. But she and Mary Noonan had talked, their beds head to head in the darkness. Mary Noonan who arrived after the Christmas of second year, a late boarder. A girl who seldom spoke in the daylight hours. A girl whose father had died suddenly over the holiday, the nuns said.

Where is Mary Noonan now? They kept in touch till marriages took them to opposite ends of the country. Mary Noonan who had been a friend but whose story had given her nightmares for years and is reappearing now in these frosty woods. As if she needs it. God knows, she doesn't need it now. That voice, that country voice coming, one night, out of the darkness.

'You know my father died at Christmas?'

'The nuns told us.'

'I found him.'

'That must have been terrible,' she'd said, having no idea how she'd deal with even the thought of her own father's death.

'It was Christmas morning.'

'Jesus.'

'I never told anyone here about it,' Mary Noonan had whispered. 'You wouldn't tell, if I told you, would you?'

'Course not.' And she never had.

'He was always on the piss,' Mary Noonan had told her, rolling on to her tummy and whispering quickly. 'He kept selling fields and drinking the money. Long as I remember our farm was always getting smaller. One day a field'd be ours and the next day someone else's cows'd be in it.'

She remembers nodding in the darkness, rolling on to her tummy, finding the light of Mary Noonan's eyes, wanting to reach out to her but not daring.

'Last year there was nothing left to sell but that didn't stop him. He'd be off for days and then I'd find him asleep in the car on my way to school. He'd be halfway down our lane. And then he went on the piss on Christmas Eve and didn't come back. Christmas morning my mother sent me out to look for him, to get him home, not to let him near the church in case he'd make a show of us. As if anyone didn't know already. For fuck's sake, everybody knew.'

Even now she remembers her chill at Mary Noonan's directness. It signalled something awful.

'The car was at the bottom of the lane,' Mary Noonan had said. 'But he wasn't in it. I opened the door. His overcoat and short coat were in the back seat. I went down the lane, on to the main road. I thought he might be walking ahead of me. There was no one else around but it was getting bright. I could hear the wind humming along the telephone wires. I always try to make out the sound, to hear the people talking, to hear the voices in the wires.

45

I can nearly hear people talking all the way from America, saying "Happy Christmas", and things. Do you ever do that?'

'No,' she'd said.

Mary Noonan laughed quietly. 'Well, I do. Anyway, I saw something, on a pole a bit down the road. It was kind of like a shadow till I got closer and then I saw it was a person. I thought it was a chap from the telephones fixing the wires but then I saw that whoever it was was hanging from one of the rails that's nailed across the top of the pole. I couldn't see the face, it was turned away from me, but I knew who it was. I screamed and screamed and then I ran, past our lane, to Parkinson's. The two lads drove back with me. When they saw him, one of them said: "How the fuck did he get up there in the dark?" And then they reversed the car and brought me home. They told my mother. She said nothing. After the guards came they cut him down and the ambulance took him away. The guards drove us to my uncle's house. When we passed the place there was nothing left but tyre tracks in the grass and a bit of rope still in a knot on the crossbar.'

And then Mary Noonan had been quiet for a while. Finally she'd spoken again. 'He was a bollocks. I'm glad he's dead.'

He might have been dead for his daughter but the unseen man had not been dead to *her*. Most nights that term she dreamt of him, dangling from electricity poles on her road, in the school grounds, even in the dormitory. Sometimes, in her dreams, she was trying to untie a knotted rope from the bar on the end of her bed. A thick black knot that could never be undone. She had woken sweating, the sound of Mary Noonan's quiet breathing at her head. Eventually, the nightmares faded. Until now.

The children are dancing on the summit, waving their arms, urging her to run the last forty yards.

'Come on,' they're shouting. 'Come on, come on.'

And she is running.

He is jogging through the woods, as he does every morning. Sometimes the long way round, sometimes the straight run to the hilltop and back again. This cold, dry morning he feels good. He is rested. His head is clear. He is running well, ready for whatever ambushes the week has planned. His strides are easy and sweeping, his feet bounce off the frosted grass. It's as though his body is floating above these legs, above legs that are younger and faster than they should be. His breath comes out like diamonds. The sun is genial in the gaps between the trees. It's glint and haze and glint and haze up through the trees to the brilliance of the hilltop.

He rests, breathing deeply, looking out over the smocked countryside, picking out the landmarks – the moat, the power station, the sugar factory – and then he's off again, down the steepness, his strides controlled, loosening into the mottled forest and along the wide avenue until he is out into the car park near the road.

Monday morning car park, after the night before. Wads of sodden tissue in the grass after the late-night couples on the way from the discos and bars. He slows to a walk, knowing the corners under the trees, counting the discarded condoms. This is something he does every morning now. Seven this morning. The scattered rubbers with their bulbs of dull semen give him hope. Reassure him. There is life out there, still going on. Passion still running wild. Couples are still fucking in cars, their mouths locked together, coming noisily, quietly, without caring. As long as this goes on, the struggle continues. He starts running again, across the car park, on to the road, towards his house.

xii

She's lying in this bed, in this room, in this house. His house. A house she hardly knows. It's late in the afternoon, the day after Christmas, and the light in the sky is helpless. This is an eastern sky. Her bedroom looks on to a western sky – lighter and brighter later. But this has nothing to do with the feeling inside her. Sufficiency. Satisfaction that they've finished, that she's come, that their bodies are apart. She feels easy. Rested. And certain that this will never happen again. She has no regrets about her generosity to him. Just certainty.

She remembers other times when they made love, when they fucked – in the weight of a hot open field the summer they married; in the kitchen while her parents talked upstairs; under a railway bridge in a blizzard, their bodies boiling in the freezing afternoon. She's not surprised by the distance of all of this. Why shouldn't it be distant? Those were other people. She closes her eyes momentarily, opens them again, turns the bedclothes back and steps away quickly. She finds her clothes in the dusk, prepares to leave. Already she's thinking of something else. Something more important now.

Suddenly he's awake, completely awake. The woman's pale skin is gone. The large beautiful eyes are gone. The breasts, pressed against the dress, are gone. As soon as he's conscious he remembers these things and as soon as he remembers he's aware of their absence. It all happens in an instant.

The screen hisses mesmerically at him. Rubbing his eyes, he pushes himself out of the chair, presses the 'off' button on the TV set and then the 'rewind' button on the video. Later. He'll return later to the would-be lovers in the summer wood of *A Month in the Country*. Later.

Outside, the winter afternoon settles grimly. Inside, the fire is a collapsed purple parachute on the grate. Is it the ash or the dusk outside? These faces. Faces pressed against the wire of some death-camp. Deep eyes calling but he hears nothing. He sees them speaking, trying to tell him something. Trying. To tell him something that must be told. Must be heard. The eyes like dulled lovebites, peering. He hurries into the kitchen and lifts the phone. He listens. Nothing but the monotony of the tone. No language. No voice. Nothing.

He stands in the cold kitchen, scanning the wilting Christmas cards, listening. Willing someone to speak.

i

'What did you want doing that for, with a lovely house, a lovely home? Would you not get together, the two of you, sort it out? How can you turn your back on all of this? We went through this, you must remember that. Times when I was on the batter and she'd raise hell and rightly so, but we got through it.'

'It's not easy for a woman to start again. It's all right for you but you should think of the other side. It's all right for you to walk away.'

'The kids won't thank you for it. You might think it's all as smooth as ice now but by God they'll see it otherwise. Wait till you see what it does to them. No one will be laughing then, I'm telling you.'

'All the outside influences, that's what I blame.'

'And that fellow. Are you bent by any chance?'

'You can only swim so far against the tide.'

'For Christ's sake, you got through the hard times, what're you doing now? It's downhill all the way.'

'We counted on you. We always thought you were solid as rocks, we never saw this coming. You were always there to be relied on. I can tell you this is some shock.'

'I can only hope they won't despise you in the end, that

this won't put them off the rails. That's my only hope for you.'

'Why don't you leave it for a while, see how things go? You owe these years to the kids.'

'It's not the same when you close the door on your own, no one else to share a house. It's not the same at all, you never get used to it.'

'How do you mean things'll be all right? They won't be all right, how could they be?'

'Every couple goes through things like this. You have to give one another enough room to get out of the way. But that doesn't mean throwing in the towel. You don't just turn around and say, "That's the end of it." Not with children, you can't do that. Jesus, you might as well lay them in a coffin as that.'

'All the work the two of you put into the place. It's all right talking about this, that and the other but it'll never be the same again. You had your noses out of the wood, kids well on their feet.'

'Too much time spent with other people.'

'Listen, you'll hear it all. They'll say you couldn't ride him, wouldn't ride him, wouldn't let him ride you, that you were riding half the town. They'll say anything.'

'You'll be kicking stones out there, with your feet in the fire.'

'No one will ever trust you again. No one. No one trusts a woman who can't keep a family together.'

'Do you know how lonely it is? Do you know how

hard it is to start again? I think you've had it too easy.'

'Take a holiday, a bit of time apart and you'll come back like it was new.'

'The kids might look like they're OK but in a year or two years, it'll surface.'

'I hope this doesn't catch you when you're least expecting it – you could go down when you're least expecting it.'

'Listen to me. If you had no choice, if you had to work this out, you'd find a way to sort it out. Wouldn't you, in all honesty? I don't want to be critical but you would, wouldn't you?'

'Things'll never be the same, don't tell me nothing's changed. Every fucking thing has changed. Everything.'

ii

He sits, waiting for the traffic to clear. Cars and vans and lorries backed up from the railway gates. He turns the key and the engine dies. He rolls his window down on the dry day. Not spring yet but getting there. And then he notices a woman at the surgery gate and something about her look tells him everything. He feels the pain again. The pain from a long time ago. A different kind of distress. A suffering he could only marvel at, about which he could do nothing. All that pain, spread over him across the childhood years, is here in this one face now. All of it in one morning. The doctor may have put some name on it, prescribed something for it, calculated some time for it but the look is there and he is terrified. By this woman's pain and by his own. Her face says no.

He sits in the jammed traffic. She stands by the surgery gate. Both waiting.

In the late afternoon, just before dark, she is walking past the hoardings around the town hall. Her eye is taken by the neat black graffiti on the newly painted boards:

'Ger loves Sally so fuck off & leave them alone.'

She smiles. For a moment she considers stopping and completing the haiku. She searches for something appropriate.

That night, in bed, she rearranges the words in her head:

'Ger loves Sally so
fuck off and leave them alone.'

She sleeps and wakes.

In the electric lit bathroom, she writes the words, just beside the mirror where the children won't see them.

'Ger loves Sally so
fuck off and leave them alone.'

And then she adds her final perfect line.

'Dante. Beatrice.'

*

iii

She stops the car on a wide stretch of roadway, turns off the engine and sits in the quietness. The rain darkens the door of the day, insinuating itself into the bare bushes on the roadside. One of those days when it isn't raining but there's rain everywhere. She winds down the window and listens to the songless road, the leafless sighing and sucking of the trees. And then she notices the gulls circling above this inland countryside. She gets out of the car and walks to the breast of the railway bridge. The gulls are suspended above a blue tractor, hanging effortlessly as the tractor ploughs its way up and down the sodden fields. A kiss of elation touches her heart. The birds flagging a new season, the plough burrowing for something that will come good.

She imagines the washed blackberry flowers climbing this bridge. She sees a day with the tar swimming on this road. She remembers a shoeless afternoon, carrying a prized poached trout from the river, wrapped in her white handkerchief. What age was she then? Younger than her daughter is now. She is back cycling on a late summer day, dismounting at the foot of Mullaghcreelan to walk the steep three hundred yards, and two fox cubs, mottled by the capsizing sun, are rolling on a bank beneath the trees.

A car slows at the foot of the bridge and comes up the hill.

This, she knows, is a new year. The electric wire above her head is singing, the trees are beginning their wombing push.

The car passes. Two faces peer at her. They see a woman leaning against a parapet, watching a blue tractor turning the earth inside out. What don't they see, she wonders? They don't see the bruises on an uncertain heart.

He hates the random way that March deals its moods. The sudden slapping rain as he races from the car and fumbles for the door key in the dark. And as the key turns the rain stops. He steps inside this house that was once his home. The cat follows expectantly. Why else should he be here, who else will feed her? He flicks the kitchen light, finds a tin and spills it into her dish. He leaves her eating, wanders through the house, drawing curtains, switching on lights.

Back in the kitchen, he lifts the cat, strokes her, carries her to the door and puts her down in the garden. She looks at him and then saunters away. He goes back inside and closes the door. He is standing inside an empty house. Not so long gone but long enough to be uncertain. He feels the need, the need to stay. It would be good to stay the night, he tells himself. Good for passers-by to see a car outside. No one will know.

He walks through the sitting room and pauses outside the closed door of a bedroom. He dares not open it. That is not the place to sleep. Not now. Not any more. He walks into his son's bedroom. The light from the hallway is a dim sheet across floor and bed. Slowly he takes off his clothes. Very slowly. He stands naked in the middle of the room, uncertain. Then he turns back the quilt and slides into the cold sheets. He stares at the ceiling. There is nothing in his head. Only the fact that he is here again. He looks about him, at the walls covered in maps. Scotland. Iceland. The United States. Reproductions of medieval maps. Kilkenny. Galway. A hand-drawn map of this town.

He closes his eyes to blot the picture out, the curving coloured streets. This house. A huge red arrow pointing to it. He begins to shake. A terrifying coldness rocks him. He breathes deeply, evenly, trying to control himself. He breathes in. Breathes out. Breathes in. Deeply, deeply. The soft smell of Olbas oil comes from his son's pillow. He lays his face in the scent, in the pillow, in whatever there is. He hears a noise in the room. The sound of his own, deep, breathless sobbing.

iv

She watches her daughter standing among the daffodils in the garden. The child is lost somewhere, unaware of the flowers about her or the trees budding above her shoulder. She stands in her bedroom doorway, wanting to walk across the garden and wrap her arms around her daughter and pour her love over the child. She wants to keep on pouring until every crevice in every bone is oiled with the love she feels for her.

But she is afraid. Afraid the love may fall like a weight on the child. Afraid her daughter may take this pouring as something else. Afraid some iota of the doubt the child's father thrives on may raise its smiling head in her daughter's life. Afraid the warmth may be lost.

She steps quietly out of the doorway and begins to cross the lawn. The child turns to her, watches her approach and then opens her arms to her mother.

The small boy's question comes back to him hours later.

'If you had three wishes and you couldn't wish for three more wishes every time you got to the third wish what would you wish for?'

He reconsiders now. For you, for her, for us, for happiness, for courage, for escape, acceptance, certainty, a new car, an old car, a dog, a tidy garden, a welcoming home. Peace for the world, joy for the world. Understanding of the world. Some way of finding a wish to begin with.

When you're old enough, he thinks, I'll explain this to you.

v

He cleans his house thoroughly. He rearranges the photographs on the shelves. He spends a long time planning

57

where he will plant the cherry blossoms. Next year they will bloom here. This house is everything he wanted.

Today he hates it.

She wakes from her dream. She cannot remember anything other than the terrible fear but now the sun is up. She closes her eyes, certain that when she sleeps she will not dream again.

vi

Early in the morning he starts work on the shambles of a garden. The rambling half-acre that was part of the initial attraction. Now it's a battleground scattered with the implements of war. The lawnmower abandoned near the gate, victim of the clumped, hummocked grass that has been uncut for years. What seemed wildly pastoral a month ago is now merely wild.

And somewhere in this chaos his son has seen the possibility of a football pitch. By the weekend there must be order. He leaves aside the clippers, abandoning the tedious business of trimming for the more satisfying task of slashing his way through the nettles behind the shed. The air grows tart with the smell of broken nettle stems. He sweeps the blade through the air. Again and again the acid breath comes from the shadow of the wall. Sweep and slash and sweep and slash and then, in the corner of his eye, a red gash on the end of the blade. Bird? Animal? He mouths quietly, Shit.

58

The scarlet flitters from the hooked blade, somersaulting back into the grass. Peony rose.

He breathes again.

Overgrown peony rose slashed and cut with all the rest.

Early in the morning she drives out of the empty town. Mist squats in the fields. She turns off the car radio. Who needs news on a day like this, a day already gathering heat. Bad news has no place in such a day and nothing can match the still beauty of the morning. She rolls down her window on the warm breeze of the countryside. Glancing in her mirror, she smiles at the two sleeping children behind her. Washed and dressed and ready for the day ahead and already exhausted. And just as well – sufficient for the day is the intoxification thereof! Her smile becomes a quiet laugh.

Then a bird touches the windscreen, its wings brushing the glass as a leaf might, rising as a leaf might in the draught of the passing car. Rising and rising and then, in the rearview mirror, tumbling and falling into the road.

She slows and stops the car. She checks that the children are still sleeping. But everything has happened so gently, sweep and fall of ounces of feather, that nothing breaks their dreams.

She walks back along the road quickly. The green and yellow bundle lies on the black tar. She bends and lifts it in her palm. Still warm, the skin unbroken, the wings and feathers all in place. Breath of life, she thinks, and she breathes on the bird.

The feathers come to life but not the bird. She lays it in the thick branches of the roadside hedge, its head resting on a wild woodbine flower. Green and yellow too.

vii

She's standing in the kitchen, drying the last cup. The afternoon house is quiet. Empty. Not an empty loneliness, more a silent satisfaction. Hot, quiet, solitary. Nothing is oppressive. The emptiness and silence amount to nothing. The cup in her hand is shining. As a child, when it was her turn to dry up, she'd shine each cup and plate and saucer and put them high on the dresser and then she'd sit and admire them, the light spangling across them. Now she hangs this final cup from a hook on the shelf and watches its gentle swing.

Reaching up she pushes the kitchen window wider. The laburnum is still yellow on the lawn. She notices a leaf on the window sill, behind a candle. A dead leaf that fell from a sprig of something or other and lay there for a long time. She lifts its rusty shape and her heart falters. The sunshine has ironed a perfect leaf on to the light wooden sill. She hunkers down to examine the leaf, the fractured pattern of its edges.

He knows this is one of those days. He must keep moving. He must keep doing. He draws the sheets from the bed and piles them on the floor; strips back the pillowcases;

pulls the duvet from its cover and piles the linen into a bundle, ready for the wash. He pushes the windows as wide as they'll go. Stooping, he takes three paperbacks from the floor beside the bed. A cup is glimpsed under a chair. He reaches in and takes it out, expecting a ribbon of tea around the edges. Instead there is the orange dye of his daughter's night time drink. Her lips against the rim, fair hair thrown back, her eyes. Her mother's eyes.

viii

She lets the photographs slide across the kitchen table, sixty photographs spilling from a wallet made for half that number. They skid and flicker in the sunlight from the open back-door, a shuffled pack of queens and knaves and jokers from another August afternoon. A dry church porch, its top carelessly clipped; grey leaves from the previous winter still swirling in the frozen print; helianthin; familiar faces. Dead faces. Her own face. She studies it for a long time. The same face. A different face. And his face. Was there deceit even then? In the smiling, wily eyes?

Her eyes move across the other faces. The obviously dying, the surprisingly dead. Was it an afternoon like this one? No. Much less sunny. Much cooler. Some things, at least, have improved. She smiles a dry smile at the thought.

*

The stones spill out of the plastic bag, across the Formica table of the rented holiday home. The children are hunkered on their chairs on either side. They begin sorting the stones they want for their collections. He takes one stone from the pock of sandy colours. A stone the size of his bent thumb. A round stone that reminds him a little of the earth seen from space. One side a smooth blue, the other a cracked grey. He puts the stone in his jeans pocket, thinking he will give it to her when he returns the children.

Later, walking the clifftop, he takes the stone from his pocket. It looks inconsequential. He puts it away. Tomorrow he will skim it across the calm sea-water and then regret its loss.

ix

He stands in the yellow kitchen, looking across the garden. His eye is drawn back from the hills beyond the valley, back from the valley itself, back to the branches of the twisted evergreen behind the garage; from the mass of the tree to the figure in the flat branches at the top. His eight-year-old son squats in these branches, his green peaked army cap pulled low, his binoculars tight to his eyes scanning the fields for something, someone. For a German infantryman or a Japanese sniper. Or for something less real. For something unspoken and unspeakable at his age.

He cannot avoid the thought that his son is there, in the

62

high branches, for some reason other than play. And then he remembers his own boyhood hours, spent alone in the Rocks or in the furze bushes on Rice's hill. Simply for fun. But it wasn't simply for fun, was it? It was for something else. For escape from something, he knew that. And in search of something never found. He looks at his son in the tree and sees two boys. One is mortally wounded by what went on around him, the other is still capable of laughter. He leaves the kitchen and crosses the garden. He waves to the small boy and then begins climbing through the raw branches, emerging on to the plateau of soft palm. He sits by his son, looking out across the fields.

'There,' he says quietly.

The small boy peers through the binoculars. 'Where?'

'There, behind the gate, far end of the field. Look. See. There.'

Together they watch the sniper who doesn't yet know they have his measure.

It's late, very late, and the rain is still falling straight on the glass roof outside her bedroom window. It has been falling like that all evening. Straight and hard. But she has only just noticed, now in the silence after a night of bitter talk. After explanations to people who have no right to expect explanation. People who expect because they qualify as family, extended family. People who spent the hours explaining why they were right and she was wrong. Children. Family. Home. Friends. The years, what about the years, you can't undo the years, they said. You can't just sweep them away. The words came, like the rain, straight and hard and bitter.

In the end, in order to escape, she faced them down. 'You don't mean children or family,' she said. 'You mean yourselves. What this will do to you. Isn't that the point of it? Well, isn't it?'

And they looked at her, like horses watching a road, nodding, seeing but incapable of sorting one thing from another. And when she left they followed her to the car, asking her back. She drove away, leaving them in the porch light, the vellum faces following her departure.

Now she gets out of bed and opens the connecting door into the conservatory. The rain batters away. She slides back into her warm bed, lies in the almost darkness and remembers a night when she went out, long after midnight, and stood naked in the pouring rain, letting it massage her hair and skin and eyes.

But not tonight. Tonight she is too tired for that. She lets the sound of the rain go on falling in her head but she is too tired to make anything more of it.

x

Suddenly, this afternoon, there is sun. The apples feed off it. They flicker and flash in the garden. She takes a bowl from the garden and goes out to collect them. Each one is fingered, tested for hardness and ripeness. The chosen few are lifted carefully, turned and snapped from the branches.

She smells their smell from her fingers. Each one is placed carefully in the bowl. Sometimes the sun off the skins is blinding. She chooses the last apple carefully and takes it to where she can sit in the hammock and enjoy the sharpness of its flesh. She lies back, savouring the taste of her garden.

A question comes, creeping from some corner, brought out by the pungent apple smell: What, after all this time, will it feel like to kiss an unfamiliar mouth? She cannot imagine its taste. She recalls the terror of adolescence, facing the first kiss. The expectation and trepidation. They return but there is a sunny anticipation, too. She closes her eyes and smiles and knows hope, again.

There it is, among the brittle sycamore leaves. The house. The long remembered house where, as children, they stole apples. The house whose orchard was only part of the temptation. The orchard in which the woman walked every afternoon. The woman whom they watched from the sycamores. The woman who walked so casually among the apple and plum and pear trees, her sallow hair piled high. They had sat in these trees, three boys, waiting for her to go inside, waiting to steal the apples. Watching the woman who walked the afternoon. And here is the house again, among the curtained branches, here where he left it thirty years earlier. And he is surprised.

He stands among the trees, not daring to walk any nearer, not daring to check whether the wall is still intact, the orchard still standing, the house still alive. These things matter but they are too precious to be tried. He stands quite still and remembers the woman walking the orchard and wonders, as he has often done, whether her husband came at night and took her hair down from its nested curls, feeling it plunge heavily through his fingers, or whether she unpinned it for him in the yellow light of their summer room. The sun catches his eyes and he is blind for a moment and then the wind hoists some leaves across the light and he can see again.

Were they even in love, those people in the house? Perhaps not. Yet how could anyone not love that woman in the orchard? In the end it didn't matter whether her husband had been as fascinated as he by her hair, by her slow walks through the garden. There had been a fascination. That was all that mattered then, and is all that matters now.

an october saturday

This is the morning after my forty-first birthday but that has nothing to do with it, that is coincidental. Just an October Saturday. When I began to wake some sense told me there was light beyond my inseparable eyelids. I knew, too, that I had to open them to reaffirm my existence, but they wouldn't open. It wasn't tiredness, it wasn't an infection and it had nothing to do with the day before. That had been as sober as every other day in my life, you'd be the first to attest.

I could hear with a clarity that frightened me, hear everything from the garden and the woods, hear sighs of things I had only imagined and the clearer the sounds the greater the need to open my eyes. It became a matter of life and death. My life and your death. Something in my brain told me to relax, to stop fighting and let go. It didn't say you'd be out there but that was an unspoken part of the attraction. Something else said that there's no coming back, that this isn't just about dipping my toe, that this is the real thing.

I wanted to see, of course I did. I wanted to go out into whatever blue yonder there is and then come back. I wanted both sides but I was afraid and so I held on, forced my eyelids apart, dissolving the glue of death. I believe that. I believe it was that close. And then suddenly my eyes were open and it was morning and I was in my bed and there was sunlight through the porous curtains. I was petrified and appalled at my own cowardice.

Were you?

Hardly, I suppose. Perhaps it was you who urged me to hold on. Perhaps you knew how great a disappointment I'd be in paradise.

The sun is pouring into this yellow kitchen, except that it isn't yellow any more. Apple-white is what the tin said. Apple-white it is. Through the window I'm watching the toy tractor doing its lengths of the dry field, turning remotely on the headland, ploughing all day long.

Did I say yesterday was my birthday?

I did, but I just want to reassure you that the fact has no bearing on all that happened this morning. Don't put anything down to that. That's pure coincidence.

Now, yesterday morning, that was something else. Cramming phone calls into half the time they might other-wise have taken, trying to get the decks cleared for an early lunch. Friends waiting. Just three minutes, I said, just one more call. I need to check an address and then I'm ready.

Your mother's voice on the phone. She stopped me in mid-sentence and told me.

Four years. I couldn't believe what she was saying. Jesus, I said, and then, again, Jesus. Chilled beyond the cold clean day outside my office window. Four years and I'd never had an inkling. It seems obscene. To have been that close and then not to have sensed that you were dead. It leaves no room for the flattery of soul-mating.

I'm sure you'd nod and smile at that.

The stove is roaring like a train, the open damper sucking flames from the damp logs and gulping them up in the chimney. But I don't really hear it, not the way I heard things this morning. And I don't see the dry weight of winter on the roses near the garage. I do, however, see the sun on the rocks by the river. I can't remember the name of the river and I can't remember your dog's name but I think I remember everything else.

I know that in the beginning I'd make lists of things to talk about and stick them in the dashboard locker of the car. I remember the plastic dolphin dancing above your bed. I remember the musky smell of your skin and hair. And I remember the day with the sun on the rocks near the river. You were wearing a pink dress, the pink of wild mushrooms. I had never seen you in a dress before. You were coming more than halfway to meet me, I was to find that out. And your skin smelled of musk. So did your chestnut hair that curtsied to the faint flowers on your dress. No hint of winter then. And we were far enough from people and circumstances and expectations to be safe. There was no need to weed anything out of that afternoon.

But, for all of that, I wasn't prepared for what you said.

We were sitting on the rocks and the car doors were open behind us and you said you thought we should get engaged. I was in love with you but I would never have dared such a suggestion, so I said nothing.

You don't want to, you said.

I don't have any money, I said.

You laughed but there was no sweetness in that laugh I heard.

I mean I don't have any money for a ring.

You laughed again. This time it sounded right. I'm not talking about marrying yet, you said. I'm not talking about mortgages. Your voice was light. I'm not even talking about an expensive ring, you said. I could ask my mother for a loan. I'll say it's for a dress. She wouldn't mind but if you don't want her to know. She wouldn't mind.

I'm sure she wouldn't have. But there never was a ring.

I've sat here for the past half-hour and I still can't fathom why. I could hazard a guess, from twenty years away, that my fear had much to do with it. I was in awe of you. So much so that I never gave either of us a chance. But I was in love as well. We both saw how far we'd have to come, that afternoon, and we both wanted to but wanting and doing are different things. And if you were waiting this morning, you'll have been let down again. Except that there's more to consider now, my kids and things. But you know that. You were the one for plunging in while I weighed the consequences. Well, mostly, but not always. Always is unfair to both of us.

Once, one night, there were no lists, no hesitations, no weighing possibilities, and afterwards you were the one in tears and I was the one who stopped them. I think it's fair to say we were in love. Isn't it?

See. See, out there, the blackberry leaves have gone as red as they can go and the sun is lifting the weight of the frost from the long grass at the garden's end.

We have very little to regret.

sisters

I remember this clearly, the way the day peeled strips from the dark eastern sky. I was downstairs by then, filling the electric kettle with water and that sky was in the kitchen window. From the sitting room the sergeant's voice came and with it the silences when my parents had nothing to say. It can't have been much after five in the morning.

It was twenty to five when I heard the car in the yard. I knew it wasn't my sister's car. This one came in too quietly. Perhaps, I thought, someone is driving her home but no one ever had so why should she allow them now. I looked at my watch. Twenty to five. I squinted through the quarter dusk and saw the light on the roof of the police car. Immediately I turned on my bedside light. The sergeant must have seen it come on because he waited in the yard, without knocking, until I came down and opened the door. And then he just shrugged and I knew.

He came inside and we talked in the kitchen. He sympathized and then he gave me the details of my sister's death. His words were rain on ice, warm rain, spring rain.

He'd been here before with other versions of this story but this time the facts were simple – a car, a tree, a dead woman.

'Maybe we don't need to give your parents too many details, you know,' he said.

'Was there anyone else?'

'No. Looks like she fell asleep and that was it.'

He saw my smile. He laced his fingers behind his head, unlaced them again and let them fall.

'She was drunk?'

He nodded.

'I think I'll call my parents,' I said. 'I think they should know now. I think they'd want to.'

I went upstairs and knocked on their separate doors and told them that the sergeant was downstairs.

'It's about Jane,' my mother said. She looked frightened.

My father was more to the point. 'Is she dead?' he said.

They came downstairs together, I noticed, for appearances' sake, even in these circumstances. Wrapped in their dressing gowns. My father's thin ankles in the space between his slippers and pyjamas. My mother's face more gaunt than ever. It was strange, standing in that twilit room while this middle-aged couple floated down towards us, this couple who seemed not to be my parents at all. I was reminded of times when Jane and I would come down these same stairs, dressed in my mother's clothes, playing models, and be applauded by these same people. But now the only sound was the sergeant clearing his throat.

That was when I went into the kitchen to make some

tea and listen to the gaps between the sergeant's words. And while I watched the fingers of the day appear I knew there might be a terrible sadness in the other room, an absence I could do nothing to fill. I knew that twenty-three years of life had suddenly disappeared. It was like stabbing on the vacuum pedal and seeing the flex disappear. Suddenly there was nothing left but the stolid plug against the side of the vacuum. Nothing left but a body to identify. I would drive past the tree she had hit and go to identify my sister, and yet all I felt was relief. I concerned myself with setting a tray, arranging mugs, pouring tea. I had no part in any sadness just as I would have no further part in coaxing my sister past our parents' room. No more hours of trying to talk sister sense. No more trips to pull her skewered car out of gateways and ditches. No more waiting for what had arrived. No more of that shit. That was over and I felt no guilt, none whatsoever.

Outside, the cows were grazing the field at the end of the lane. I opened the window wide and suddenly there was colour in the fields and garden. A colour that was no more than gauze.

No more false alarms, I thought. No more talk of clean sheets while we sat in her room playing the old records we danced to as teenagers. No more talk of how close we were, of how sisters must stick together. No more lies and denials. No more expectations that half a dozen scratched and crappy records can fix up everything. No more of that, not now, not any more.

The sergeant tried to keep talking while we looked into

our tea but there was nothing left to say. My mother thanked him for coming to tell us, thanked him for taking so much time. He stood up, sweeping his cap into his hand, sympathized again and then walked with me to the door.

'Come down when you feel ready,' he said. 'Any time. Don't expect it to be too bad. Thirty seconds. It'll be all right.'

I waited until he had driven out of the yard before I closed the door. I wanted to feel the sun on my face.

As I went back into the sitting room my parents were going upstairs. The sun was slopping through the window on the stairwell, soaking their backs. They looked so thin, transparent almost, walking up those stairs together.

I took the mugs, still full, into the kitchen and ran the hot water over them, swilling the weakened tea into the sink, and then I left them on the side to dry. I remember thinking that the four mugs would remind me, when I came back down, that this was not a dream. This has happened, I thought, and other things must happen, too. I thought about getting dressed and going in immediately to the morgue, getting it over and done with. I went upstairs to shower and, passing my mother's room, I heard voices, but not in conversation. I stopped and listened. I knew my parents were in my mother's bed, making love, something they hadn't done in ten or twelve years. I stood there, listening, not out of any sense of voyeurism but rather out of a sense of deliverance, of redemption, a shared sense of release. The unspoken terror that had linked us all to the possibilities of my sister's life was gone. I smiled for my parents' freedom, and for my own.

Outside, before I got into the car, I stood perfectly still, becoming part of the flawless morning. It was a better day than Jane deserved. But this wasn't her day anyway. This was our day and it had nothing to do with her. The land was alive and the world was singing. I sensed a celebration. I listened for the faint sounds of my parents in bed. I was free and I was happy.

the second epistle

I could come in anywhere on this story, now, couldn't I?
And you'd still know what I'm talking about. The others
mightn't but you would. But it's better, if we're to get
anywhere, to get back to basics, strip away the irrelevance.
Get back to the point of departure. That seems an appropriate analogy, given the circumstances of my writing this.
So here we go.

I'm a man, in a train, on a journey, through snow.

Those are the facts. Don't pin me on the order of
importance just yet. They are hard facts but in need of
rearrangement and this is as good a time as any. No rush,
no fuss. As far as appearances go. Look at me, the picture
of calm. A collected forty-three-year-old man. Greying but
not too quickly. Well dressed – corduroy trousers, casual
shoes, good shirt, nice sweater, jacket. Weekend case on
the overhead rack. Book laid casually on the table. Pen in
hand, writing. Notes for a sermon. Ah, so he's a priest?
Fine.

Now, let's get the order right.

I am on a journey. The train is not essential. It has a certain importance in that eight weeks ago I made this same journey but, then, by car. Out of Dublin, through wet, Friday, midland towns. Heavy traffic. I was travelling to bury your husband then.

You were there in the hospital mortuary. I led the prayers. I drove my car behind yours to the church. I stood with the local curate and prayed. I stayed in a local hotel. I concelebrated the funeral Mass. I stood at the graveside. I had lunch with you and your family and friends. I drove back to Dublin. I telephoned the following weekend, to check that you were doing all right. I waited.

And then I began to write that letter, in my head. I put it on paper and rewrote it and, then, rewrote it again. I made a final copy and, suddenly, realized it was on presbytery paper. How ludicrous it looked. I was glad of the excuse to do it again. This time it was better, tighter. I sent it in the Christmas post. It seemed to me that the season might make it more acceptable. If the worst came to the worst it could be ignored. What card? What letter? you could say. No, it must have gone astray in the Christmas rush. I left you an out. I left us both a way of escape.

Anyway, to get back to the point. Last time I took the car. Now I'm travelling by train. You'll meet me at the station. It may be snowing but you'll get through without too much trouble. Big car, the jeep if necessary. No, the car will do. The engine quietly humming in the car park, a tape running, the smell of real leather. When you hear the train pull in, you'll walk on to the high platform and stand in the falling snow, waiting for me to come up the steps in the yellow light.

The snow is not as inconsequential as it might seem. Pasternak would have written it in. You told me once he wrote it in for you. It may resurrect the risk of Christmastime, the willingness to risk. May. Might. Could. Can. This whole bloody thing is becoming disjointed. Back to basics.

I am on a journey. I am in a train. It is snowing. No, that isn't really essential. It has bled the landscape of light and variety but it isn't important. Regroup.

I am on a journey. I am in a train. I am a Catholic priest. It is snowing.

I am a priest. I perform the functions. I am the central cog in an organization that runs things, does things without being a thing. I'm the chief bottlewasher. My house is home to a telephone, a fax machine, a photo-copier, a thousand forms, a hundred meetings. I keep the committees going. I provide references. I do things – baptize, give communion, marry, bury.

I'm a priest, I do the work, I wear the collar. Sometimes.

And if all of this goes wrong, I'll go back to being that priest. I may take a deeper interest in something or other, the balance may shift, the emphasis may alter, but I'll still do all of those things. I won't take to the bottle. You thought I already had. When you got that letter in the Christmas post you telephoned straight away and asked if I'd been drinking. And I thought, if you had the courage to acknowledge what I'd done, I must have the courage not to hide. I wasn't drunk. I was just careful about some phrases in that letter. Careful, in the end, to include them. When I finally rewrote that letter, on plain paper, I made a point of saying everything.

I began with what? Your father's farm. My father always called it the English farm. He meant that it was neat, the hedges were trimmed, the headlands cut, the driveway well kept, the trees healthy, the yard clean. And just to prove that I was sober, honest, going for broke, I'll say it all again. That way you can check my face for honesty. If honesty is the appropriate word. Whatever. You can check my face as you sit in the car and read this.

The driveway to your house was smooth. I could cycle it in fifty seconds flat. Not a pothole. Chestnuts over everything. And the yard was always hosed. No muck.

I racked my brains to be sure that there were no variations, beyond the two I wrote about, but there weren't, were there?

Sunny days. No, dry days. Dry days we played tennis and afterwards drank tea in the kitchen. If your mother was away we went up to your room and lay on your bed. As the summer dried out I kissed you harder and harder and my hands felt for your breasts through your tennis dress. Your arms were wrapped around me, holding me on top of you. But that was it.

Wet days we put on coats and boots and crossed the fields, down to Lynch's wood and lay down under the blackthorn tree. The most secluded spot. That most secluded spot. Was it the weather, the place, the freedom, the way your hair piled back on your duffle-coat hood? You were more forthcoming there. Forthcoming? How bloody formal can I get? This is not a reference. You were more responsive, more emotional. Your hands responded, sometimes deliriously. I'd roll away, out of your frantic reach, to keep from coming. Two summers of that kind of passion. And then nothing more.

I wonder where a vocation sprouts from that kind of adolescent soil? I kept every card, letter, photograph and note until the week of my ordination. Hopkins would have been proud of me, a great fire in my room on that last free Sunday afternoon.

Were you happy with what you got, with your share of the power and the glory? A farm as good as your father's, a decent man, a comfortable life? It probably matters in the end. No children. Did you both roll away as I did on those afternoons in the wood? You're right, none of my bloody business.

For now, I've left them the house, the car, the fax. I've taken a week off. Too long, not long enough? I've gone out for a walk and I'm hoping never to go back.

Does the passion of those tennis matches that ended when your mother left the house survive in any corner of your heart? It needs to. And what about the willingness to take me to your room? We need that, too. It was never you who rolled away, remember?

What was it you said on the telephone last week? 'We really need to talk.'

Do we?

landscape with three figures

I gave birth to a child. On a summer morning, in a bright room with windows open, and I imagined the butterflies were dancing, though they told me it was too early in the morning for butterflies, that the sun wasn't hot enough at that hour to entice the butterflies into the air. But I will tell my child, when the time is right, that there were butterflies. Of course there were. On the light breeze that came through the open window at the other end of that huge room. And beyond the window were the Swiss lakes and the white mountains and the sky. No traffic. No buses squealing and juddering down Holles Street and Merrion Square. None of that. I'll tell him. None of that, not on your nanny. Sunshine and breeze and butterflies and a look of bewilderment in his eyes. In my little darling's eyes. And no one else, once the doctors had done, in that gorgeous room. Just him and me, and the summer swimming in the air, the light dancing, the butterflies waltzing crazily. No pain. No trauma. He came so quickly. So quickly and quietly, my sweet baby. Bewildered but laugh-ing. My dear, sweet darling. My love.

When I'm not driving this train, or sleeping or walking to or from the station, I'm out in the yard, the long yard behind the house. Out there and as like as not I'm standing with my hand out straight, straight at the elbow, and feeling the quivering body, the pumping heart, the little muscles tightening, watching the brilliant little eyes. And imagining the tiny brain whirring, getting itself geared up for the journey. That's the only bit that's beyond me, the only bit I can't tune in to, the only bit I don't feel inside me. I feel the rest, everything else. I feel the thrill and the loss when my fingers uncurl. For a second there's freedom but the birds don't take it. For a second you're not holding them and they're not going. And then the bird takes it, flies up. Up, circling, finding that something that I can't tune in to, finding whatever it is that separates them from us. The something that's beyond us. Up. Dangling at the end of some long piece of string in their brains. And then the string snaps them to attention. And my pigeons fly.

People talk, and talk for hours, about the most ridiculous things. Talk seriously about the most abstract things. Make you think they know what they're talking about. Relate someone else's opinion like it was their own experience. Bullshit. I heard a crowd one night, in a quiet pub, talking about the phoenix rising. About what that really meant. About the experience. Not what it stood for but what it actually meant. What it said about courage and feeling and hope and closeness to the earth. As if talking about it was of any worth. As if any of them had any closeness to the earth, beyond mowing the lawn in the summertime. All these semi-detached people talking about finding themselves in nature, about rising as the phoenix did. I leaned across and said to them, Losing yourself is what the natural world is about. Losing yourself in it. Anyone will tell you that, anyone that knows. Ask some farmer about meascan mearai.

They looked at me, angry that I interrupted, not a bit interested in what I was saying. Not knowing what I meant and not thinking it worth their while to enquire. The phoenix! God bless their childish hearts.

The platform lights are yellow and the fog is yellow under them. Yellow with October but cold with November. Nothing like the heat of summer when I cradled my baby. There was heat in the window space and there was a unique light in the sky and the days were blue. And then there was the smile of my sweet, sweet darling. It all added up to July. Give me July. Give me then, not now. Give me the smallness of his body to warm, the lightness of his bones to make me forget this bitter cold.

Sometimes the single beam of light from the front of the train reminds me of the track my birds set themselves once they've got their bearings. I imagine something inside their heads latching on to that line, pointing to one place and taking them home, mile by mile, in spite of everything. The lightness when they're gone, in the seconds after they fly, is one thing. The gap when the feathers fly is one thing but the flutter when they come out of the sky, stepping down the invisible stairs from wherever they were, is another thing entirely. It's like the Holy Ghost coming down into my yard, into that long, narrow yard. It feels that way, every time. Wings and feathers and the tired eyes on them. Coming in from heaven.

These people run from the rain. Wrap themselves away from the cold on a night like this. Shelter from the sun when it shines. Look out at the day instead of wearing it. Talk about but never do. Watch television programmes about the Arctic without ever putting their foot in a snowy wood. You see them flying off to sit on manufactured beaches but they never slipped into a river in a dusky summer. And then they talk about the phoenix rising from its ashes. Would they know the bird on sight? Would they know the feel of ashes?

I like this train, this time of night. I like the way the carriages glide past me, empty. I take my choice of seat. I take my time and choose the seat I want. Empty as an early bus. I choose my seat, arrange my things, stow my case on the seat opposite. And then I walk to the restaurant car and buy coffee and saunter back to my carriage. My space. My light. My face staring back at me from the black window.

The worst times are when I snap back from my pigeons and find I'm breathing diesel into my lungs. That's when it's worst. The smell in the cab. The oil on everything. No air, no light, no sky. Just the smell of oil and the tracks parting in the light and the line that goes on for ever. And the fog sometimes and the ghost bridges that come out of the night and disappear again. And the creaking of the engine when all I want is to hear the pigeons sleeping. All I want is to stand in my yard and listen to the almost nothing all around me.

Lilac in the early summer and the smell of water, there's a smell from river water, even from fresh water. But the best they can come up with is roses. If they want roses let them go out and find dog-roses, real roses. Subtlety that only nature can come up with. Let them go and stand in a ditch of dog-roses until their senses are acclimatized. Forget the vulgar standard roses that pass for flowers in the walled-in handkerchiefs they call gardens. Mollycoddled. Lilac and river water and dog-roses. There's smell, there's colour. I'll tell you what their problem is, they think talking is as good as doing and it isn't. They're cunning but they're not strong.

Sometimes I'm overcome with a terrible sense of foreboding. I become ill at ease. I find myself constantly watching for things. I find myself becoming wary of people. I dislike it when people impinge on my space but this becomes more acute. Troubles seem to pile up all around me, waiting to happen. I sense that things are about to happen but I know I have no control. I know trouble is out there but I can never quite pin it down. It frightens me, that terrible waiting, that knowing but not knowing enough. I see the troubles in the unpredictability of people. I know my family thinks me unpredictable but that isn't in the way other people are. People don't fear me. But I fear them, I am terrified of the sudden explosions of violence among people in the streets.

I wouldn't say birds are better than people. Sometimes people think that's what I'm saying but it's not. Birds aren't better, they're different, and there's a lot of the differences that I like. What they give is different. And when they die the gap they leave is smaller but deeper. Sometimes the gap can't be filled. There's dead birds I remember better than people. I wouldn't say that out loud but it's true. I can remember two birds, at least, that I held in my palm and their lightness was the weight of the world. I got on with things but I never forgot them, the gap was never filled and I never wanted it filled. I remember them more fondly than anyone that ever died on me.

This mightn't make sense but bear with me. The other day, between trains, I went into Dublin to buy something and I was walking in Georges Street and I saw this couple.

They were in their forties and they were kissing on the corner of the street. Laughing and kissing one another and then they went their separate ways. Husband and wife. They looked like husband and wife. When the woman got to the corner of the street she looked back and I knew, just from her face, that she wanted to get a last look at the man because she loved him. A couple of seconds afterwards the man looked back. His wife was gone by then but his was a different look. She was gone but he kept looking, checking and double-checking. And then he doubled back and cut across the street and into a hotel. And there was something all wrong about him. There was something all wrong in the way he was looking.

When my birds circle and look back at me there's nothing wrong in their look. They don't mislead me. They check once and then they fly straight and fast as they're able. That look says, I'll do the best I can. And I look back at them and I think the same, do the best you can. Do your best and, then, come back to me.

I know this field. The railway bridge and the cottage on the opposite side, with the doorlight that throws red and yellow and blue colours on the red-bricked wall. A two-storeyed cottage, all lit up at night. All reassuring in the daylight. Solid. But it's the field I know best. I love this field. I love lying in it, winter and summer, watching the trains going by. The big light, the roaring carriages and their lights, the fading tail-light on the guard's van. But the train is only part of it. I love the field for itself. In daylight it's the same as any other field. More or less square, in grass, hedged. Road on one side, railway on the other, other fields on the other two. Ordinary. At night the flatness is intimate. Lie anywhere in this field and you can hear a heartbeat. In the dark it puts on sensuality, exudes abandon. I know it has this power.

I once took a woman I knew out here at night. She parked her car in the gateway and we walked in here. She didn't question the wisdom of our taking off our clothes and leaving them in the middle of the short grass. She let me take her clothes off and then watched me while I took off mine. She didn't say, Let's come back in spring, this is October. She walked with me, around this field. Sometimes we stopped and kissed. I could feel the hardness and coldness of her body. We stood, naked, on the embankment while the passenger train passed, flashing and wrenching and straining while we stood silently. She didn't say, This is like Eden. Nothing so trite.

After the train had gone we went back into the centre of the field and we could smell the grass and feel the earth and the small pebbles under us. We kissed and touched and fucked and when we had finished she lay on me and I felt the hot stream gushing from her, warming my belly and my thighs. It was her way of saying this field is a good place to be. I want whatever this field, this land, can give me, she was saying.

She felt nothing. He saw the figure but only in the last few seconds. It came from the right, running along the side of the track. Too late, too late. The timing all wrong and then the figure swerved, a naked man or woman, hurtling on to the line, one foot on a sleeper and then gone again, breasted by the weight of the locomotive, lifted like a bubble and burst along three hundred yards of line.

The woman watched herself in the black window, watched her face for a long time after the train came to a halt. And then she noticed figures passing along the embankment, men with torches. And she noticed the fog had cleared. And then the ticket-checker passed through her carriage.

A short delay, he said.

She closed her eyes and the butterflies were dancing in the white room and the window was open on the brilliant hot Spanish countryside. A fan whirled steadily overhead and the baby lay on her tummy, his mouth on her brown breast.

For a moment there had been a gentle swooping into the air and then a running movement again and then the locomotive lifting and a hot sweetness in the mouth. Like the hot, wet smell that night in the field. But this was blood, not piss. And there was blood splashing up from his torn knee and then tumbling again while the locomotive rolled him along the sleepers and the packing stones. And then he was tumbling away to the side and the first sensation of pain came, in the back of his neck, as he came down on it in the dry grass of the embankment. And then there was the scream of the train as carriage banged against carriage and then everything slowed and ground.

And his heart was pumping, pumping out the blood from his knee, from his mouth. The train was slowing but still going away from him. The red light and his heart pumping as though the pump would never stop, even though there was no blood left to pump.

days

Graham Boylan always had a red face and as he's got older it's got redder. Every time he comes home from England his face is redder and his wife's hair is more platinum. And every time he calls for me I know it's going to end up the same way. The way it ended up last night. Him pouring double brandies into me and then drawing a crowd around him and telling them what a wonder I was. It's always the same. I know it word for word. Sometimes a bit more loud and a bit more colourful but the gist is still the same.

It begins with him asking people in the bar, whatever bar we go to, if they know who I am. And they look at him as if he's not the full shilling. Course they know. Peter Hill. Born and bred here. Had a shop open till three years ago. Widowed five years.

And then he says – But do you really know? And they look at him as if he has two heads. And then he launches into it. Do you know this man put this fucking town on the map when no one ever heard of it? he says. Do you know this man's name was sacred (that's what he says) across Ireland and England? Do you know if this town was worth anything there'd be a street named after him, there'd be a plaque somewhere?

And they laugh. But that just makes his face redder and his voice louder. Fuck's sake, when half the world was shitting itself over Cuba we didn't give a damn because this man won the National title for the fourth year in a row. And no one went the distance with him in this country and only two men in internationals. He could've turned pro. They were queuing up to sign him. I seen cars driving into this town, men with cigars going into his shop, trying to sign him. This man was my hero, he was hero to half the country and no one did anything. It depends on the likes of me to come home here every year and try to light a fire under the fat arses of this town. He was my hero when I was ten and he's my hero now and I'm not afraid to say it.

And then he demands that I take out a cutting I have in my wallet. A write-up and a photograph of me posed in shorts and singlet, gloves held up the way I'd never hold them in the ring.

Last night he had his wife and another woman in tow. Her sister, I think. Slimmer than his wife but every bit as good a looker. And brown haired. A nice woman. But, anyway, his wife got in the act this time.

He talks about you everywhere he goes, she said. There's no one he doesn't talk to about you, no one.

She brought the photograph over to show to her sister

and when she brought it back she winked at me. Pity I wasn't around then, she said. Your muscles and mine would've worked well together.

He's not past it yet, Boylan said, and he slapped her arse.

Nature calls, she said. I'll be thinking of you. And she toddled off to the ladies with her hips swinging and her blouse open to the navel.

And when she was gone, Boylan started on again. Put this town on the map he did and no one gives a damn.

He's not dead yet, someone said.

That broke the tension.

Right, Boylan said. Right. Still hale and hearty. What age are you, Peter?

Sixty-one, I told him.

And looking forty-five, so watch your wife, someone else said, and Boylan laughed and slapped another double brandy on the counter in front of me. That's what did the damage. I can laugh about it now, propped up in bed, but an hour ago I was sure I was for the long box. Too much drink and too fast. Never again. Free drink is one thing but not when it's being lorried into me.

My car is out in the church yard. My new car. Dark blue and lost in the blue-black night. It's more November than March, isn't it. Hopeless. I always found November hopeless. Not even Christmas could save it.

There's no light from the church windows now to glint on the roof or windscreen of the car. Only the rain running down the broken gutter and splashing on the chrome bumpers and the new number plate. The car is lost until morning. So am I. And they'll find the car first, when they come to open up the church. Same sacristan who missed me tonight, who didn't see me slumped between the pews. Stricken.

Stricken? Stroked? Stricken, I suppose. I should know after all these years. A little while ago I thought I heard a voice. I thought it was someone singing in the church. A man's voice. Singing 'Rule Britannia' but the words were all wrong and sometimes the tune became 'Greensleeves'. But who could be singing in the church, in the dark at this hour of the night? Once I got that straight I knew the voice was inside my head. And then it was singing again, only this time it was a woman's voice. My voice. Soaring like I could never make it soar:

> While thou shalt flourish great and free,
> The dread and envy of them all,
> Rule Britannia, Britannia rule the waves.

Rule not rules. It makes a huge difference. All the difference in the world. Imagine having the strength, now, to sing out loud, to let my voice echo around this black church. Wouldn't that be marvellous. To do that would be such a release. Any song. Not a hymn but any song. The less Catholic the better.

Once, someone said to me that she expected, when she was seriously ill, that her mind would become concerned only with the pious and the straight. But she found herself as interested in the decadent as she ever had been. Even the face of death didn't frighten her from the things she longed for. Is this a little the same? This desire. To sing. To sing something that would never be heard inside these walls. Is this something the same?

It was one of those nights with no closing time. We were there till well after one and then we stood in the door, sheltering from the rain. Boylan and his peroxide wife and her brown-haired sister and me.

Someone passing by said, Hello, Peter. And Boylan's wife said, in her Birmingham accent, No way he's forgotten here. And Boylan started off, again.

They know him, he said, but do they appreciate him? Do they know what he done for this kip? Do they know that? Do they? No fucking way.

Most of them weren't born then, I said, to calm him down.

But he wasn't having any of that tack.

No way, no fucking way, he said. Enough of them were. I've been away the best part of my life and I didn't forget. There's enough of them here to remember. That's a cop out, Peter. I tell people everywhere what you done, don't I? The peroxide woman nodded. Her sister looked bored and beautiful. She was tapping her toe on the pathway.

You want to be getting home to bed, I said to her.

She smiled and said nothing.

Can we drive you home, love? the peroxide woman said to me.

96

I laughed, and Boylan laughed. Easy knowing you don't know the town, he said.

I just live across the street, I said.

I was that drunk that I thought of asking her sister if she'd like to come back with me. Just as well I didn't.

Boylan made me promise I'd come out with them tonight. We'll get to fuck out of this town, he said. Drive to Athy, go to Clancy's. Go over the times, right?

Right, I said.

He took one of the women on each arm. The peroxide blew me a kiss. Her sister smiled and said, Nice meeting you.

You too, I said. I even checked the knot in my tie.

They walked across the square and got into an English registered Cortina. I crossed the street and Boylan bipped the horn when he passed me. I waved. I was nearly home by the time they turned at the top of the street. I came past the post box, checked that the street was empty, I always do before I open the door. It was. Green in the traffic light. I pushed the door in and closed it, immediately. Better safe than sorry. Always better safe than sorry.

Did I slide or did I fall? I mean did I glide gracefully between the pews or did I thump like a sack falling over? I don't remember falling at all. I remember the pain that seemed to be ripping the inside out of my head and I knew, in an instant, what was happening, but I have no recollection of the fall or of how long I was unconscious. I was lying on my right side when I woke, my dead side.

I searched the side of my face for blood. Strange to touch without feeling. Like when you wake in the middle of the night and your arm is dead. But now it really is. And my leg and God knows what else. So much dead. So much still functioning and so well, too. But how much is dying? How much is getting ready to cross the line? Is the right side, the dead side, working gradually across? It doesn't work that way. I know that. If it comes it'll come in another blinding snatch and that will be that.

I found no blood. Just a bump. Not too big but just above my eye. It's too dark to have any real idea about the damage that's been done outside. Inside is where it counts. And how long ago? I came in here at what? Ten past eight. No idea how long I've been here. It could be nine, it could be twelve, it could be almost morning. My watch is strapped to my dead arm, strapped under me. After nine. The church shuts at nine. Locked. Bolted. Silent.

No blood. Just the bumps. Some pathologist will have thirty seconds' fun with that before he moves on to the real business of the day, sawing my head open. How many nights have I sat, cooling people's foreheads with eau-de-cologne, knowing that in twenty-four or thirty-six hours they'll be sawn apart? Enough to know what's there for me. Could be a day away. Could be a month. Could be years for all I know. Could be here, alone, in the big empty church. Now wouldn't that be strange.

Here on the floor where I knelt as a child, the wooden floor with the flat grey stones that marked the priests' graves. Here in this church that frightened me as a child. Where I knew I had to do something to banish the fright. Where I'd hurry in and race the stations and be gone again. Where, finally, I overcame my fear by hiding in the organ loft until the place was empty. And then I peed down the wooden stairway, squatted at the top and thrilled at the trickling stream running down, step after step. Thrilled at the smell that was rebellion.

Whenever I needed release I'd come in here and do that. Half a dozen times in childhood and adolescence. The smell of pee. The sound of the swoosh on the timber floor. The sight of the yellow water running across the floor and down the brown stairs.

No one ever knew and no one ever knew that I was no longer afraid of the church and the square gravestones in the floor and the dark stairs and the shadowy statues and the burning sanctuary lamp. And once I was free of fear I could come in here without any fear at all. I could come because I was at ease, because I wanted a few minutes' quietness, because I felt it held no power over me. Everything was all right. Not that I spent every Sunday sniggering about what I'd done. I didn't see it as something like that. It was therapy. Childhood therapy, before I knew what therapy was. And whatever I got from it then, whatever release, I got something greater when I grew up. It made me feel relaxed in here. The way I feel relaxed now. No point in panic. There's nothing in this place that will do me harm. Only what's going on inside my head can do me harm.

It always takes me a while to acclimatize to the dark of the hall. I don't hurry it. I let the things down there come out of the darkness in their own time. No point in rushing them. No good ever came of that. And last night the stairs came out of the darkness the way they always do if I give them the time. And when they were there I walked up them. Slowly. Nine steps, a little landing and then two more and then I leaned in and switched on the light and there was the bed, the chest of drawers, the wardrobe and the pile of English Sunday newspapers I keep for looking over when I fancy a bit of tit.

This used to be a store-room, when the shop was open. Briquettes and coal out the back shed; groceries and hardware in the side rooms and sweets up here. But I cleared it out and brought the single bed down and put in the small wardrobe and the chest of drawers. It's a warmer room and handier. Saves me seventeen more steps up and back. I like this room, always did. A good big window out across the yard. In the autumn I can see the leaves on the creeper going yellow and in the spring there's the few snowdrops at the far wall and in between there's the frost on the shed roof and the sun on the grapes.

Last night, when I got in here, I crumbled down on the bed. It took me a while for the head to clear before I pulled off the boots and socks and then I reached under the bed for the pot and I remembered I'd left it down in the yard when I emptied it. As soon as I missed it I was bursting for a slash.

I undid my trousers, turned off the light and pulled up

the window and pissed out into the yard. And I remembered one night when I was really scuttered, standing in the sitting room upstairs, bursting, and opening up the front window and pissing down on to a motorbike that was parked outside on the path. I didn't give a fuck whether I was seen or not. And half an hour afterwards I heard it starting up and I laughed, thinking about some poor fucker riding all the way home sitting on my piss.

Do I really smell that smell or is it my imagination? The smell of new car. The smell of leather and plastic. The smell that says new when you open the door. Of course, it's in my imagination. When that smell goes the newness is gone from a car. It's still in mine. Reassuring. Won't it be strange, though, to have someone else driving that car. Less than a month old and finished with, useless. A little like the smell of coffinwood. New. Fresh. Shining. And finished with life. Finishing with life.

I've often thought of myself lying in this church. In a coffin. At the head of the aisle. Wondered about the sounds and smells of the night-time church. About the terrifying silence inside the coffin. I always assumed that I'd be aware, despite death. Always felt I'd be cut off, beyond communication, of course, but not beyond observation. Always felt I'd be aware of the desolation of that night before burial when the crying people are gone and there's only the corpse left in solitary misery. Sixteen hours laid at the altar, waiting for family and friends to come back. Waiting for the inaccuracies of the final homily. I never dared take it beyond that. Never contemplated the longer darkness and deeper silence of the earth.

Even as a child, sitting at the top of the gallery stairs, waiting for the pee to stop running from step to step, the thought of being brought back here in death occurred to me. Even then I thought my little act of restlessness would in some way staunch the flow of banality that some priest would pour over my remains.

And now I don't care. To be left here dead is one thing. To be left here dying, presumably, by a hurried sacristan is another altogether. I never planned on that, it never darkened the door of my imagination. Perhaps the church has had its revenge. Who in their right mind would want to lie dying fifty feet from the closed door of a tabernacle behind which squats an unforgiving Christ?

Too true, dear nurse, too true. There is no escape for him or me. He's locked inside and I'm trapped down here with slim chances of making it to the morning. Whenever that comes. Whenever that is.

What time?

What time.

That smell, again. Of new car. The clean dashboard. Sweets in the pristine ashtray. The mileage counter still only in double figures. The plastic covers on the spotless seats. All that is mine. And the rain is shining the blueness for the first light of the morning. Who said there's no beauty in mechanical things? I've never bought a car that I didn't think beautiful when it was new. The paintwork will be like Bluebonnets in the morning. And when John Behan comes to take the car to the garage that fresh, strong smell will meet him when the door is opened. And only sixty-seven miles on the clock. Will the young curate mention that? Use it as a warning, not to be certain, for death has a habit of popping up like an unexpected traffic warden. Sixty-seven miles, my dear people. What is it? Nothing. On a car that could have done a hundred thousand without any trouble. But the car was not the problem. Life was the problem. Or the lack of it.

There, young whippersnapper, is your sermon. Clever enough even for you. Sixty-seven miles. Fifty-eight years old.

Clare Moore was dedicated, outgoing, always had a smile. Spent her life nursing the sick. There isn't a house in this parish that she hasn't been in. Let us remember her as a woman who served her people well. As a child of this village. But not as a rebel who peed down the stairway of the church.

If I could only get my hand free, see the time, know what's expected of me.

When it was, when it was whatever time it was, I woke with a bursting pain in my bowels. I tried to relax, to ease myself out of it and I did, to an extent. But then it came again and I knew I had to get out of here, get down to the lavatory as fast as I could, as ever I could. If I had the time. I could feel the insides churning around. When I got it a bit easier I got out of bed and pulled on my trousers and coat and shoes. I thought about squatting over the newspapers in the corner but then I thought I'd make it.

I fucked that dead bulb in the hallway. A young fellow that lives at the far end of the street promised me, months ago, to bring in a ladder and put a new bulb in. And I must have asked him a dozen times since but never a sign. What am I saying? It was last Easter he promised. And every time he's going to be up before the weekend.

I had to stop in the hall and hold on to the banister and brace myself against the pain. And then I shuffled along in the dark, along the passage between the stairs and the shop. That shop down there that's full of rotting chocolate and crystallized sweets and cans full of beeswax candles. I never go in there any more. I hear the scattery noises on the polished counters and I know the damp is spreading and I know I could let it but I have this feeling that as long as it's left alone nothing will change in my life. I closed it because it wasn't making ends meet. Someone else could come in and rip out the two counters and fuck the bacon slicer into a skip and put in strip lighting and turn it into a small supermarket or a video shop but where's the point? It's not meant for that. That's the way I see it. So let the mice have the run of it and let whoever wants do whatever they like when I'm gone. Anyway.

I pushed on the switch in the kitchen and the beetles ran in every direction across the flowers on the lino, back into their black holes under the skirting board. As soon as I had the back door open I felt sick coming up in my throat and I had to stop again. Wait. And it passed. I leaned against the concrete wall and spat out as much of the taste as I could. I went to walk down the yard to the lavatory and turned my heel on a dead mouse that one of the cats dropped. The bastard. I pulled the twine in the lavatory, it turns on the light. And then I closed the door and pulled down my trousers and pants and just in time. I had to clutch my knees with the pain, rock myself back and forward to ease it. And then the diarrhoea burst out of me and the pain nearly blacked me out and then it eased off, gradually, until I could sit up straight again. But I knew there was more pain coming. I tried to put it out of my mind. Tried to think of something else. Of the small green grapes that still come out on the woody vine against the wall. Of the turfy smell in the outshed, years after the last bale of briquettes was sold. I always loved that warm smell in there, just to walk in and get the smell of turf.

I should have brought another coat down, to drape across my knees. It's always cold down there at night, even in summertime. And then there was another bout of pain and that eased. And then another but not nearly as bad as the first. I knew I was going to be all right. I took a quarter sheet of newspaper off the nail on the back of the door. There was a story on it about a young fellow that was up for stealing a car battery. I went to school with his uncle. When I finished that I thought I was all right. That I might chance coming back up here. And then the pain started again, shooting up through my bowels. And then they cleared, with one rush. It left me weak but I knew I was finished. I pulled the chain and opened the door a few inches to air the lavatory. That's when I thought I heard something, and then a girl screamed and my skin went cold, real cold, sweaty cold. I sat there, one arm raised, holding the chain. A car door thunged, there was another scream but I recognized it for what it was, a drunken laugh. And I heard voices in the lane behind the yard wall.

'Don't be too long,' someone said.

'We won't,' a chap and a girl said together. And then a car started up and drove off. The fear went out of me, like the pain. I sat there, I don't deny it, listening. Listening for some sound in the lane. I could imagine the girl with her back to the wall, my wall, not twenty feet from where I was sitting. I opened the lavatory door wide and listened as hard as I could. I knew they were out there. I could see her with her skirt up around her arse, see your man with his tool drove into her. I could imagine the whole thing. And I wanted to hear something, some little gasp or cry or word.

But nothing came back across the wall. Not a sound.

How long have I been talking to myself, singing to myself, reciting to myself, remembering out loud? God knows. How long have I gone on, afraid to be silent? Afraid that there might be nothing else if there was a silence. Afraid that one silence might bleed into another.

I never trusted March. It has a way of turning on you, coaxing you out and then sending sleet. And this is more of it. There I was, running around all day, house calls. Chatting and laughing. Showing off the car. Putting the world to rights for Mrs Hearns and Mrs Grey and Mrs Connell and Mrs Richards and the rest of them and they'll probably see me down.

Oh, she was here the day it happened, seemed to be in great form, it came out of the blue. You can sing it. Or the odd one claiming they noticed that I was a bit grey or a bit green or not myself or forgetful or something else. Some nonsense.

That was always one great thing about March. Going up Connell's drive and watching the snowdrops and then the daffodils in March. I would have been up there tomorrow or today, is it today? Whenever. All the big, loud bunches of yellow holding their own against the rain and the wind. Proud as punch. They're the boyos to give March the bum's rush. And Mrs Connell in her big, high bed asking me how her flowers are doing and me telling her they're fine, wonderful, better than ever. And there she is, what, four years stuck in that bed? Longer probably. I thought I'd see her down. Who'll bring news of your flowers now? Someone, no doubt, someone else.

And who'll look after my own few clumps? Someone else. I can't think who but someone will, won't they? Maybe the children will come in and take them in fistfuls, clear the place in half an hour. Maybe. Maybe not. Oh, Jesus!

I keep thinking of that peroxide one in the pub, she'd be the kind to go down alleys and lanes. Knickers around her ankles in short order, I'd say. Even now, I'd say, she's not beyond it. Imagine her tits tumbling out in your hands. Jesus! I'd prefer the other one, though. A bit more class. Quieter. What age is she? Forty-five maybe. Size her up tonight. Get a chance to look her over. More than likely she'll be sitting in the back seat with me. If she comes. They'd never leave her behind. No, she'll be there. Loads of time. Look her over.

God be with the times when the wife was still alive. She'd cut the eyes out of me if she thought I was looking at anyone like that. Even in the shop, I'd have to be careful how I looked or when. To be caught was deadly. For fuck's sake, I don't think I ever saw her naked, standing up in the buff or anything like that. It was always done out of sight. Hoist the nightie in the dark and pull it down when the job was done. Hard to imagine she was the same girl that climbed in the window of my bedroom when I was working on my uncle's farm. Climbed in and left a gladiola on my pillow while I was out in the field. She was seventeen then and everything that came afterwards in our married life contradicted that one thing. She'd burn me with a look if she thought I was studying some young one in the pub. Silence for a day. But it worked. You get in the habit of doing what's expected of you. If you don't break loose in the first few years you're fucked. Silence was a great whip. Let me know where I stood. Twenty-four hours of that and the lesson was learned. Well learned.

Jesus, when I think of it. In this very room. Once and once only but if she ever found out she'd have closed the door and that'd be that. I nearly forgot that. This very room, when it was a store. Must be the bones of thirty years ago. The young nurse. What the hell was her name? Shit, won't come back to me. She was here a year or so at the time. Came in looking for a carton of lollipops. It was during the polio immunization, that's right. They were trying to get all the kids to have the needle and they were giving a free lollipop to every child that got it done. She came up to the store with me, to see what size carton she wanted. I mean, I knew her. She was in digs the other end of the town. She came into the shop a couple of times a week. She had great tits. I always thought that. Anyway, we came up here to get the sweets and we were chatting away and she caught me looking at her. There was no getting away with it. Her blouse was open down a few buttons and I was staring and she caught me dead. No denying it. I thought she was going to give me a bollocking but she said nothing, just took my hand and put it inside her blouse and held it there, the back of my hand against her bra. I couldn't go on looking at her tits and I could hardly stand there looking into her face so I kissed her on the mouth. She didn't seem that interested and, at the same time, she kept my hand against her, pressed hard against the material of her bra.

In the end I told her we better stop, that my wife might come up. Even then, even when I said that, she seemed to want to keep my hand pressed into her. I had to say it again, say I thought I heard someone, before she let me go. Then she stepped back from me, took the carton of lollipops and went down the stairs in front of me. She left the sweets on the counter and paid for them. Like nothing had happened but there was a peculiar look in her eyes. She came in again whenever she was passing but she never made another move and I made sure to keep my eyes where they should be.

If the wife had known, suspected. I was thinking of that earlier on. Thinking about the wife.

I gave up listening for the pair in the lane. I was just getting ready to come back up here and the door was open and then I saw a shadow in the arch of the briquette shed. Whoever it was seemed to be clever enough to stay beyond the spool of light from the lavatory bulb. I tried to hear the breathing of whoever was there. I could feel the pain starting again and I leaned over to close the door, lock it, and the watery, stinking mess ran down my leg. I had to sit down with the pain. The shit oozed on to the seat and then it came rushing again and I had to put my head on my knees to keep from fainting. I could feel the bones through the skin of my knees. I was sure I'd pass out and I kept waiting for whoever was in the shed to come up the yard and bury a hatchet in the side of my skull. I had to see who was coming so I pushed myself forward and looked straight down the yard. It was deserted. The light was shining on the paraffin tank, on the rusty blue. There was no one there. I was angry at myself for being such a fucking coward. And then I thought it might have been the wife's ghost, hanging around in the shed, watching me, and that didn't frighten me at all. I just started laughing.

Maybe she's come back for revenge, for me feeling that nurse's knockers, that's what I was thinking and that started me laughing even more. I laughed for a long time because I no more believe in that than I do in the man in the moon. She's dead and I'll never see her again and I never even think about her, much less miss her.

And then I stopped laughing and I thought about myself. Sitting there in the cold in the lavatory with stinking shite down my legs and all around the seat. English women is right! What would they think if they could see a shit-covered geriatric on a dirty toilet seat, with a yellow photograph in his wallet? Carrying it around like a bullet in a soldier's head. Taking drink from gobshites and watching their wives sniggering about the bulge in my shorts. All a load of bollocks and nonsense. That's what I was thinking. I'd be better off found here with a hatchet whacked into my skull, that's what I was thinking. That's what I was thinking. And fuck them.

There's something about a church at dawn that makes it look medieval. Not every church. But this one. The pillars and the ceiling. I never realized how far up it is but then I haven't been lying between the seats too often either. But the grey light coming in through the windows. Not the stained glass windows. The plain ones. The ones where the light comes in straight and grey. They make the place look medieval. All it needs now is a dozen men in cowls, floating down the aisle.

It seems a lot colder since the light came up or started

coming up. As if the sun had extinguished the heat that was here through the night-time. How long will it take for someone to see my car? Someone who can put two and two together? Not too long. Not too long before the doors are opened and I call out to the sacristan. Will he think the place is haunted? Put the heart cross-wise in him.

What do I say? Hello. I'm here. Over here. Excuse me, I've been lying here all night. Savouring the atmosphere. Ruminating. Trying to work out twelve across. I thought I might find inspiration here but it didn't come and now would you mind calling an ambulance. And maybe it won't be so bad. Maybe there is life after this. Maybe I will live. I have lived this long. Survived the night. And in the morning . . . How did that go? And in the morning . . . I can't even remember what it was.

I survived the night. I will survive the rest of the day. I will.

I pulled the string on the light in the lavatory and there was a softer light of dawn about to come over the shed roof. I wiped myself as best I could and walked down to the tap outside the back door. I washed myself down and then got a wet cloth and went back and wiped the lavatory seat. And then I came back into the house and found myself clean pyjamas and boiled up a kettle for a hot water bottle.

By the time all that was done it was daylight and I came up here and lay in bed, feeling the way you do after a sickness. Glad to be getting better. Not fully back to life but enjoying getting there. That's how I feel. And I'll sleep all day and get up in the late afternoon and have a bath and spruce myself up for tonight. And I'll keep an eye on the jar. All things in proportion.

It's good to feel good, to sort things out in your mind, to sort out what matters and what's nonsense. You do that when something like this hits you. You sort it out for yourself. I do anyway.

I might die, later today I might. But I don't think I'll die here. It's almost fully light. Soon someone will open the church and I'll be taken out of here. A warm bed in a warm ward. I might die there but that's all right. The numbness won't be so bad there. The strange feeling that half your body is not missing but tacked on to you, not really part of you. You can't see the joins but you know it's separate. Impossible to describe unless you've felt it yourself.

One time, for maybe eighteen months, I was consumed by a desire for numbness, I wanted someone to suck my breasts so hard that they'd go numb. All one year and into the following summer I watched mothers feeding their children and I envied them. I wanted someone to take my nipple in their mouth and suck it. It was an ache. A real ache that went on and on. And, fool that I was, I did nothing about it. Apart from one pathetic attempt at something undefined, with a shopkeeper. I got him to feel my breast but that didn't stop the longing. It only made me more frustrated. I knew this man would never be any use to me. And I couldn't, or wouldn't, ask any other man. Or woman. I just wanted someone to take my nipple and breast in their mouth and suck it till it was numb. It wasn't a maternal thing. It was sexual. I craved it. Someone to take the longing away. I'd take my breasts in my hands and hold them there, waiting for some spirit lover to provide release but it never came. The longing just faded, very slowly, into a different kind of numbness.

It was like peeing down the stairs in this church but I couldn't reach that satisfaction. The child had her revenge but the young woman had only frustration. And the knowledge that the first brush of someone's lips across my nipples would release such passion. The knowledge that my breasts were beautiful. The knowledge that so much was waiting. And all I could do was take some shopkeeper's hand and hold it against my breast until he became embarrassed. I'd like to talk about that to someone, to some young nurse in the hospital. I'd like to ask some young nurse if she has ever felt as I did. Has she ever had a longing to have someone kiss and suck her breasts until there is no sensation left, only the absence of longing.

Perhaps I will. I think so. Let her put it down to the stroke if she chooses. If not, if she's enlightened enough to understand me, I may find someone who can answer the questions about longing, describe the sensation. Now that there's no sensation whatsoever. I feel I may be lucky in that regard. I may even live, go beyond survival. Begin again. Begin. Again. I like the thought. Begin again.

still and distant voices

I detest that old lie about memory playing tricks. Insanity plays tricks. Disease plays tricks. Not memory. Memory is hauled into shapes and versions like sacks of grain but the stuff inside remains the same. And, in the end, death comes along like a rat and gnaws the bottom of the hessian and the grain is gone. It may take time but the grain is gone.

I tell you this because the memory she has is of another man, a creation of her want. He has nothing to do with the real man. I knew the real man. There was nothing evil about him, nothing calculating, nothing despicable. He just wasn't the man that she wanted him to be. And, anyway, it was all so long ago. She was a different person, too, but she has never allowed that person, that girl that she was, to go free.

I tell you this because you need to know. You have been sucked in before. By language. By the turn of a phrase. A turned phrase is nothing more than the way the wind changes. It makes you feel better or warmer or brighter.

It means nothing. That's all I really wanted to say. And I'm not sure of the worth of saying it. But, anyway, it's said.

I hear the sound of the kettle singing on the hob. I hear the faint ticking of the clock in the hall. Hear the rolling of solid tyres in the yard. Hear the sounds of love. Hear the sounds of birth. Hear the laughter. The murmur of old voices. The singing of the young. The whisp of scythes across the fields. The rattle of milk in churns. The voices in the marketplace. The boots on gravelled paths. Sense the taste of oranges. Taste the lilac in the air. Hear her wipe a wisp of hair across her face. Her face? My face. Hear him calling in the street. The soft hug of her arms. My arms. The ache of sweat. The hardness of labour. The bugle call.

I worked in Ardreigh house, for the Hannons. I liked my work. Lighting the fires early in the morning before the house was stirring. Before the world began to stir. I was the only one stirring. In the kitchen, dining room, study, parlour. I ran the baths, drew the curtains. All these things were my responsibility. And in the afternoons I was free.

I'd walk down the Barrow track and across the Square. I'd live through the week until my day off came around. For that whole day I was free. I could forget the coal buckets and the soft cold ash. For that one day a week the dream was mine. I'd walk along the avenue and the avenue was mine. The roses in the garden were my roses. All that was mine for one day in every week. I'd rise any time I pleased. I'd take my time across the town. I'd wait for him in Barrack Street. I'd wait for his face among the faces crossing the bridge at dinner time.

He loaded barges on the Grand Canal. I know he hated the work but he did his work. He was reliable. He always said that something would arrive. I knew I was that something. Despite the bugles and the call to arms and the posters about king and country.

I'm spoiled for choice, he said, when he was signing up. Barracks, recruiting office, labour exchange, post office. Spoiled for choice.

God save the king, of course. But, God save us all, I said.

He told me to let the past go. Like a log in the water, he said. Let it go like a log across the lock. No promises, he said. Nothing. The past is dead. Remember tonight, he said. Promises are the death of things. We have tonight. I think he said all that because he didn't know what lay ahead and it was too late to ask.

After he'd gone I was in pain. I went about my work in pain. Sometimes I'd bury my hands in the silken ashes of the morning. Sometimes the world seemed to smell of dead ash. Sometimes I thought there was nothing but dead ashes in the breeze from the river. I'd pour the ashes in the snow. Grey pain. The wind blew from beyond the hedges, sweeping the snow from Aughaboura to Tonlagee. The summer was full of memories. The winter full of dead memories.

Oh, the summer. Coppered primroses on Rice's Hill, clinging on to the banks above the Lerr. Wild violets in the crannies of the rocks. Cowslips, as proud as life, in the fields behind the Cuckoo Steps. The Griese warping below Kilkea. The tongues of corn licking the neck of Mullaghcreelan. The bluebells losing their colour as the sun fell but the scent went on like a fallen sky in the night.

I should be home, I said to you that night but softly so you would not hear. I should be home three hours ago.

You showed me the gate where the dead man lay.

Lie down with me, I said, so soft you did not hear. Me with bluebells in my hat. You laughing.

Nothing to do with small nations, you said. Nothing to do with empire. Where is there a smaller nation than this town, you said. There is nothing glorious in death, you said. Death is the same no matter where. I didn't join to die, you said. For money.

You tried to trivialize it all. But I saw the importance of what you were doing and it cut me like a scythe. My best boy dressed in khaki. All those reasons for you to go. Propaganda, you put it down to that, but I knew better. Where a smaller nation than this town?

You told me once that before you left for France the chaplain came and prayed with you. He told you all to walk with God in your hearts, with light in your eyes, with hope inside your heart, with the love of God as a shield to guard you. But there was nothing before you in no man's land. Only flares in the night sky, hearts bursting with shellfire, no shield against machine-guns. The chaplain was short on words then. Only the cursing words of men screaming above the bursting bombs. I know. I know.

I can hear the sound. The sound of the universe dying. The sound of lovers wrapped around each other one last time. The sound of a man crying. Of a child in pain. Of anger. Of betrayal. The sound of your mouth in my ear. The sound of my voice in your hair. The sound of blood rushing from the mouth. Of blood in your ears. Of death inside your head. Of bitterness. Of clay on coffinwood. Oh, the sound, the sound, the sound.

I know you sought the truth in everything. You were different.

I remember that July. The breeze blowing through the saplings. The aprons of rain overhead, coming down to meet the fields. The stalks turning the saffron of the cottage thatch. And we were the lovers sneaking through the corn, lying on the ground. You pushed my throat back with your tongue. I felt your tongue inside me, inside my mouth, hard and wet against my own. We were the ones who made intense love with the skylarks spouting in the sky. And when we walked home the moon was drowned in the river. That was a strange month. Between the flowers of June and the autumn-time. There is nothing left of that month now but the voices keep on speaking your name. The sun still sweating on your skin. That was the month before sin or sorrow or guilt. The month before clocks and calendars. I wish I was lost in that month for ever, sheltering from a shower of rain. Life had not begun to falter then. Or die.

But your voice cried out of the depths to me. *De profundis clamavi*. I heard your prayer my lover. Out of the depths of hope. Of hopelessness. You cried to me.

Sometimes the night was so silent in the town that I could hear the cattle lowing out along the Carlow road. There was holly in the hall, then, and garlands on the great front door. Darkness didn't frighten me and neither did the silence of the night. Only the silence, day after day without a word from you, frightened me.

The house smelled of mince and roasting goose and sneezing logs and after the midnight service we joined the family and toasted the season and the town and the fighting men. Afterwards, I sat looking across the flooded river and watching the stars floating in the Barrow and I thought of the summer long gone and the summer that might never come.

The streets were silent and the Square was still but the river went on. If there had been a sun it would have wept in the trees. My blood was frozen in my veins and so, I know, was yours. I knew it would never be summer again. Birds would never dart in the lanes again.

I never lay down without a thought of you. I never do. I never taste wood-smoke without hope. Your situation concerns me constantly. In times of darkness I speak to your body. I whisper things into the night. Let me whisper to you now. You are my only hope. I sleep with you, my arm across your skin, my tongue in search of yours. Listen.

Listen to my other voice, even now, singing about beauty, about how a heart can waste of loneliness, about the love I have for you and draw from you. Touch me.

You. Not the shopboys and farmers in the photographs. Your face there among the eager faces, waiting for the moment to begin. Among the solemn faces in the photograph, fearing that moment. Among the fading faces. All those boys at Passchendaele.

Passchendaele. The name sings like a bird sweeping over cornfields, soars like a bird singing over the river, makes me think of dreams, like a bird soaring over clouds. Passchendaele is like a whispered love word. Soft and sensual. Like the urgent whisper in the night. In the moment of shuddering. When you are close, murmur the word to me. When you are in need say it. When you want me for yourself, breathe Passchendaele. Say it. Write it. Whisper it. Like a voice at a dark window, say Passchendaele. My dear, sweet lost love.

There was snow and a brilliant moon. You must have cursed the moon. A full moon on snow. Crossing open country. Under the remains of the hill at Passchendaele. Such light. Perpetual light shine upon you. Eternal rest grant unto you. Days of wrath and days of mourning. *Dies irae, dies illae.*

Tell me again. Tell me everything, the way you do at night when you are here. Speak that most unsatisfactory of phrases. Tell me you love me. Tell me my skin is an orchard of peaches. Tell me my hair is deep, dark chestnut blossom. Say you want to be lost in the forests of my body, to lie again in the forest, with me again, this time in a bright white room. Don't tell me there is no more music now. Don't tell me a raven is piping in the empty field in the razor wind of spring-time.

How badly I want your lips to say that phrase. Talk to me as you did in the empty church when the storm was stopped outside. I want to hear your voice in the dark chapel praying me.

> Our lady bearing roses from my garden. Our lady of lust. Our lady of the Lerr. Our lady of the Barrow. Our lady of the Somme. Our lady of the prussian dress. Our lady with old roses on her skin. Our lady of the brightest eyes. Our lady of the morning. Our lady of tenderness. Our lady of the marigolds. Our lady of the crowded market square. Our lady of hope. Our lady of hopelessness. Our lady of the chestnut shelter. Our lady of the laneway. Our lady of the singing voice. Our lady of the past. Our lady you have loved and will love now and for ever. Amen.

I am not dreaming. I am listening, carefully, for the sound of your voice. Among the other voices. I listen in the street on market mornings. Listen in the park on summer evenings. Listen in the porch of the empty church. In the stairwell of the empty house. Sometimes, in November, just as the fog is lifting and darkness hangs on the Barrow, I hear murmurs that might be whispers of wind in the ditches or water against the canal locks. Or a voice.

There is a wound through which love comes in and goes out. And through the same wound death comes in and stays. Lodges like a stranger. And bit by bit makes itself at home.

In the beginning, I saw a fleeting figure at the window. I was unsure if I really saw it. It might have been a shadow cast by an apple branch. It might have been a curtain in the breeze. It might have been despair. But, bit by bit, I came to recognize the shape of death and its particular smile. I cut back the apple branch, pulled down the fluttering curtain, accepted despair and made my peace with death. There was nothing else to say or do. We had our time. Our time was gone. There were others who sat in empty pews. Others who waited for you to walk out of the Christmas lights. Others who expected your face to peer from shuttered doorways. I had no time for that but I knew, I saw, in a time to be, us with the past abandoned like a dress. Outside the window it was snowing or the window opened on spring. The past was unimportant. Love was the importance. What did I mean by that? I meant a certain scent, your face freshened in the stream between my breasts, your eyes alive with now, the stillness before a day full with the future, your brown eyes of July.

They came alone or in groups. Their breath was dead. They passed like shadows on a country road. You were among them.

And one more thing. The only man I was ever sure I killed was one of my own. This man. This man I shot for cowardice because I was afraid not to. He gave me five letters, written the night before his execution. Each one to his mother. He asked me to post them to her, at weekly intervals. They were full of stories about how well he was doing and how bravely. I took his letters and I shot him and each time I posted a letter I remembered him. His sallow face. His green eyes. His shirt blotched red after we had fired.

over the rainbow

How do you choose a place in which to die? You know the how and you know the why but you can't decide on the where. No, let me rephrase that. How do you choose a place in which to kill yourself when you know the how and the why? But I'm not being entirely honest with you there either. How do I choose a place in which to kill myself? I know the how and the why, it's just the where that's the problem.

When I was a small boy *The Wizard of Oz* was legendary in our family. My parents had been to see it eight or nine times during their courtship and my father was forever telling me it was the best picture Hollywood had ever made. Best story, best makeup, best acting, best music, best set, best everything. He promised that if ever it came to a picture-house near where we lived he'd be sure to take me to see it.

I must have been about seven-and-a-half or eight when it came to the Ritz in Carlow and we were all set to go. I remember the evening. We were just about to leave the house, it was after tea, when someone called. Some farmer who wanted a valuation done; someone who wanted a site measured; someone who wanted to look at a house – my father was an auctioneer – and it was a question of business before pleasure so we didn't get to go. But my father promised there'd be a next time. And sure enough, a couple of months later, the picture turned up in Bob's place in Athy. But this time there was no question of going. This time it clashed with some political dinner dance or other and, my father explained, being an auctioneer in a small town he couldn't afford to offend any political party. You never knew when you'd need a favour done, he said. You never knew when you'd need a planning permission pushed through and so he never missed a political dinner dance of any persuasion.

It must have been shortly after that when my father started to tell me these bedtime stories about the Wizard – they started as simple stories but they soon grew into a legend themselves. That winter, whenever my father put me to bed, he'd tell me these stories about how he and I set out for Carlow to see the picture. But we weren't taking any chances. We left the house just after lunchtime. And we weren't travelling in the normal fashion. Nothing as mundane as a car. In the story, my father explained that we had a barge moored on the local river and we were travelling to Carlow in this. He told me how we went down and untied the barge – it was called *The*

Yellow Brick Road, and he'd always say, 'I'll tell you why later on' – started the engine and chugged down the river.

In the first adventure he told me about, we were wedged under a bridge out at Halfmiletown. The water was too high, the bridge too low. Just as it seemed we were about to be foiled again, my father had a brilliant idea. He jumped off, raced to a nearby house, returned with a shovel and shovelled rocks and clay and sand into the river, building a dam, and the water level fell, the barge scraped through and we sailed on.

A week later he came up with an adventure where we were attacked by a monster as we crossed the Mill Pond. My father dispatched him with a blow from the shovel. As he told the story, I could see the monster's huge empty eyes as it slid back into the black water.

A few weeks later a third episode was added. This time we were attacked by pirates – they had discovered why the barge was called *The Yellow Brick Road*, all my father's money had been turned into bars of gold and hidden in the hull – and I fought them off while he sneaked aboard their three-master and brought the three masts down with three huge blows of the shovel. I could hear the timber creak and snap, I could feel the splash as they dived off our barge in panic.

Each episode ended with us arriving in Carlow, tying up on the Barrow track and my father taking me ashore to a sweet shop where I was laden down with sweets, ice-cream and Corcoran's lemonade. Then we hurried down

Dublin Street and Tullow Street and into the Ritz where the lights were just going down.

Always, at that point, my father would cross and turn off the light in my bedroom so that there was just a glow from the bulb on the landing. He'd come back and sit on the side of my bed and there, on the end wall of the room, I'd see a flickering screen with Dorothy and Toto and the Tinman and the Lion and the Scarecrow and the Yellow Brick Road stretching away for miles. And my father would start to sing in his low, broken voice:

> Somewhere over the rainbow,
> way up high,
> there's a land that I heard of once
> in a lullaby.
> Somewhere over the rainbow,
> skies are blue
> and the dreams that you dare to dream
> really do come true.
> Someday I'll wish upon a star
> and wake up where the clouds are far behind me,
> where troubles melt like lemon drops
> away above the chimney tops is where you'll find me.

I never remember any more of that song because by then I was always fast asleep.

When I was twelve I was picked to play for the school football team. I was a pathetic footballer but they picked me anyway. I was put in as a half back, I think because the backs were tall and the midfielders were strong and the teacher reckoned, if the worst came to the worst, they could kick the ball over my head and keep me out of trouble. I remember rushing home, full of excitement, to tell my parents. My father seemed as proud as I was. He said this was the beginning of a great career and he'd be sure to come and see me play.

Our first game was against some Christian Brothers' school from Athy or Carlow or Portlaoise or somewhere and the team was let out of school at a quarter-past one. We marched down to the field and got togged out. I remember the pride of pulling on the number five jersey. I ran around the pitch with the other boys but, once the game began, it became obvious that I was being outplayed. The boy who was marking me was bigger and fitter and faster – better – than I was. At half-time, as we were standing in the centre of the pitch chewing on our quarter oranges, the teacher came and asked if I'd mind giving someone else a run in my place? I was surprised I'd lasted even that long.

I went and sat with the other boys on the sideline. About six or seven minutes before the game ended I saw my father arrive and stand behind one of the goalposts, talking to some of the other parents.

When the game ended and I'd togged in, I went to meet him. He told me I'd played brilliantly. I'd been outstanding, he said. His eyes were moist with drink. When we got home, he told my mother the same story. I was superb, he said, and it was only a matter of time before I'd play for the Lilywhites. I didn't tell my mother that he hadn't bothered to come and see me play. Not because I was afraid of the row or because she might be upset. It wasn't that. And I didn't tell my father that I knew he hadn't thought it worth his while to be there – not because he might be upset. It was just that even then, even at twelve years of age, I couldn't find the strength, I couldn't find the energy. I was too full of pain and hurt, even at twelve years of age, to tell him how I really felt. But I never, ever, ever forgave him for what he'd done to me.

When I was in college there were a number of guys in my year, in my class, who were gay. I always made a point of not being seen with them, not being associated with them. Once, a mutual friend of one of these guys and mine asked me if I'd talk to his friend. He had some problem or other and he seemed to think he could talk to me, that I was the confessorial type. I listened to him, I don't even remember what his problem was, and threw in whatever clichés came to mind and when he was about to leave, just by way of winding things up, I told him to be careful. I had no idea what I meant by that and neither, I'm sure, did he but it seemed an appropriate way to finish the conversation.

Waiting in the hospital for the results of my tests, I was sitting in a small waiting room. One other man and myself. We got talking. He was gay and he had full-blown AIDS. He talked and talked. He told me he'd been in a steady relationship for the previous seven years. No hanging around toilets, no going to clubs to pick people up, no promiscuity. His partner and himself had even bought a house. A small house with a little garden. A house on a quiet street. The kind of street where kids play football in the afternoon and elderly people stroll down for the papers on Sunday mornings.

He put me straight. He said, 'When you go down for the results of your tests, when you go into the office – if there's one person there you're OK, if there's two people you're fucked.'

It wasn't that he was trying to make me more nervous than I was. It was just that he had this information and he was passing it on. He'd grown up in a small village, like me. Two sisters, his parents and himself. When he realized he was gay, he said, the thing that worried him most was the fact that he might never have that warm family situation that he'd grown up in. But, when he told them, his family had been completely behind him. His partner and himself would go and stay with his parents for weekends. They'd go and visit his sisters and their families. Everything he'd ever hoped for or dreamed of had come true. And then this.

I remember walking down the corridor from the waiting room to the doctor's office and playing that game we'd play as children when we'd pluck petals from a flower and say, He loves me, he loves me not.

Walking down the corridor, every time I passed a door I'd say, There'll be one person, and then I'd pass another door and I'd say, There'll be two people. It went on and on like that – there'll be one person, there'll be two people, there'll be one person, there'll be two people – until turning a corner I bumped into some nurses and lost count. And, anyway, I realized how childish a game this was. Whatever result, whatever verdict was waiting for me, was already there, sitting in a folder on that desk. Nothing I could do – no game – could change whatever was waiting. So I walked on, knocked at the office door and went inside.

There were two people waiting for me. There were two people.

A few weeks later I came back to the hospital for some more tests and I met this same man I'd met in the waiting room. Simon was his name. It seemed like a chance in a million but then, when I thought about it, it wasn't. Not any more.

Every time I'd come to the hospital I'd call to see him. And then I started calling because I wanted to. Because I enjoyed his company. Because I was his friend. His partner was dead by then.

One weekend, about a month before Simon died, I called and took him out for a drive. We drove out of Dublin, out through the Wicklow mountains, through the Sally Gap. It was a warm afternoon late in summer. We just sat in the car and watched the scenery passing by, saying nothing. When we got down to the coast I parked the car and we got out and walked on this huge, empty beach. Not another soul on it. Not another sinner, Simon said. We walked slowly, right out on the tide-line. At the end of the beach there was a rocky inlet and we sat there and took off our T-shirts to catch the last of the sun. And while we were sitting there some emotion – but emotion doesn't do it justice – some feeling welled up in me, overcame me and I walked across behind where Simon was sitting and kissed the back of his shoulder. For a few seconds I thought he hadn't noticed because he went on sitting there, staring out over the flat sea, and then he turned around and reached out and touched the side of my face. He ran his fingers down across my neck, across my nipple and down on to my belly. And then his hand just fell away.

I kissed his mouth and his cheek and his neck. We were blood brothers.

Perhaps that was the place to die but I wasn't ready to let go.

Anyway, enough of this maudlin talk. Do you remember the summer of 1976? The warmest summer in living memory. It was also my last free summer. I'd grown up in a family constricted by rules, in a village constricted by rules and this was my last chance to break free. I headed for London. I got a job as a kitchen porter in a hotel – which meant I swilled out the piss from the toilet floors in the morning and washed the salad in the afternoons and sometimes the two seemed to criss-cross. But the money was too little and the weather too hot to be stuck inside so I spent my free days scouring the building sites for a start. After three or four attempts I came across an English gaffer and I asked him for a start.

He looked me up and down.

'What's yer name then, Paddy?'

'John,' I said. 'My name is John.'

'All right, Paddy, can you dig?'

'Yes, I can dig.'

'Can you carry the hod?' He was matter of fact.

'Yes, I can carry the hod.'

'You 'fraid of heights?'

'No.'

'All right, Paddy, we'll give you a week's trial.'

All that week I was first on the site in the mornings. No digging was too hard, no hod too heavy, no height too great, no overtime too demanding. I was twenty-four – young enough to believe in my own strength, old enough to know when not to push it. The gaffer was impressed. At the end of the week I was made permanent.

It was a lunatic summer. It was also bicentennial year and London was full of Americans who'd come over to escape the bicentenary and ended up bringing it with them. Of all nights I picked the fourth of July to go to see *The Mousetrap*. I remember sitting in the theatre at the interval, surrounded by Americans, thinking, If only I could figure out who done it I could leave happily now. But I couldn't figure it out so I had to stay to the end. After 'God Save the Queen' had been played about fifty blue-rinse Americans stood at the back of the theatre and sang 'The Star-Spangled Banner'.

As the summer wore on the weather got hotter and the shorts on the girls in the streets got shorter, their blouses got skimpier. Some time in late July a new bloke – another Irish bloke – came to work on the site. On our first day together we were a hundred and fifty feet up in the air, sitting on a steel girder, eighteen inches wide, dangling from the end of a crane, trying to manoeuvre it into place when suddenly he began to scream. 'Jesus Christ, look at the meduccets on that. Aw, fuck me, look at them, look. Ah baby, I'd be dug out of ya. Baby, come on up here, I wanna make love to you.'

He was pointing at a girl in the street below us. I kept thinking, If Jesus is even slightly offended by all of this then it'll take just one slip of the crane-driver's hand, one puff of wind and we'll both be wrapped around a cement-mixer and there'd be no more meduccets, no more fucking, no more anything, just the long brown box.

But either Jesus wasn't listening or he wasn't offended and we survived. But as the summer went on and we got higher, my friend got louder and louder. And it was always the same cant – I wanna make love to you.

On my last Friday on the site the gaffer took me out for a drink. He brought me down to a pub called The Blue Coat Boy, a traditional-looking place. We walked through the bar and into this small backroom. There were half a dozen snooker tables crammed in and twelve to fourteen blokes playing. They ignored us and we sat chatting. The gaffer told me if ever I came back to London I was to look him up and he'd guarantee me a start.

While we were chatting some music began to play and the lights came up on a tiny stage in the corner. A girl came out and began to dance. I could hardly hear the music over the clacking of the snooker balls. Then the girl began to strip. She unbuttoned her blouse, kicked off her shoes, dropped her skirt, removed her bra and peeled off her pants so that she was dancing there stark naked. But that wasn't the interesting part. The interesting part was that through all of this the blokes went on playing snooker, arses in the air, eyes on the table, not paying her a blind bit of notice.

Then the music ended, she stopped dancing and bent down to pick up her clothes and was about to walk off when, from a doorway behind us, there was a raucous shout.

'I wanna make love to you.' My mate from the site lumbered in, swept his hand across a table, scattering balls and gestured to the girl.

'I wanna make love to you. Come on, baby.'

It was that kind of lunatic summer.

Speaking of love. Have you ever noticed how easy it is to fall in love but how difficult it is being in love? I mean, if we made a list, all of us, about the things we associate with falling in love it would – with one or two personal exceptions – be the same list. You hear a song on the radio, a love song, and it seems to speak to your particular situation. You turn an aisle in the supermarket and there, at the other end, is the object of your affection. You imagine they must hear the beat of your heart. You drive into the town where they work and your heart runs amok. You see a car in the street, the same colour and make as your loved one's, and you step into the traffic to check the number plate. You telephone them on some pretext of business and you try to make the phonecall last, in the hope that they'll hear the 'I love you' in your voice. You write a letter, always late at night, and then you post it immediately because if you don't you never will. You see. It's the same for all of us.

We met through committee meetings. My lover and I. We were on the same committee, working for the good of the community. We always seemed to be the first to arrive and the last to leave and if ever we went to someone's house for coffee we seemed to be the ones who ended up doing the washing-up. We went away one weekend, to a seminar in Wexford, and on the Saturday afternoon, when our lecture was over, we had an hour to kill before dinner and we went down to the beach for a walk. Going down some steps in the rain we both lost our footing and held on to each other for support. That electric feeling when you hold the hand of the person you love. You want to go on holding it. You want to transfer that feeling. You never want to let them go.

When we got back from that weekend, I wrote one of those letters. I finished it at a quarter past two and then I went out in the rain and posted it. I knew if I waited till morning I'd lose my courage.

We spoke on the phone, two days later, and there was no mention of the letter. Had I said too much? Too little? Had I not made myself clear? You called the next day and this time you talked about the letter. You said my feelings were reciprocated. That was the phrase you used. Every cliché became a fact. I was walking on air. I was ten feet tall. The person I loved loved me.

We arranged to go away for a weekend together. I booked a chalet by the sea. It was one of those weekends when everything that could go wrong did go wrong. The car gave trouble; it rained all the time; the heating in the chalet didn't work. We spent the Saturday afternoon walking up and down the beach. It was pouring rain, blowing a gale, freezing. We went on walking up and down and up and down that beach. Afraid to go back to the chalet. Afraid of what might happen. Afraid of what might not happen. In the end, the cold and the dampness drove us back. We lit a fire, cooked a meal. We talked and talked and talked until there was nothing left to say and then we kissed. That first kiss that undammed everything. Made everything possible, probable.

When I think back on that weekend I think of the taste. The taste of the sheets after we had made love. The bitter aftertaste of wine from your tongue when we kissed.

We'd meet whenever we could. Sometimes our half days coincided and we'd make love in my bed in my room. You may laugh, you may be offended, but when we made love it wasn't just sexual or sensual or spiritual. It was like the perfect prayer. Every time we made love was like the perfect prayer.

One weekend at the end of the following summer we drove back through the village where I'd grown up, out to a hill a few miles beyond it, where I'd played as a child. It had been very fine for several weeks and then it had rained for a couple of days and now it was fine again. As we walked up through the woods the pungency of the under-growth, of the clay, of the trees, was alive. And then we came out on the hilltop, above the timber line, and everything was hot and dry and bright. The tops of the trees were about ten feet below where we sat. It was as if I could step out and walk across them, the way I'd walk through clouds in a dream. I pointed out that you could see five counties from the top of that hill.

Everything was laid out below us like a rainbow of colours. The yellow of the corn, the gold of the stubble, the red of ploughed fields, the green of pasture, the grey of the road, the blue of the sky, the hundred shades of the trees about to turn. All of this laid out beneath where we were sitting.

I turned to you and said I'm giving you all of this.

You smiled at me and said How?

I'm going to put all these colours into a ribbon and tie it in your hair, I said.

You stopped smiling. And what'll you do then, you said.

I'll untie the ribbon and let your hair fall down over your soft blue eyes.

Perhaps that's the place to go back to. To die.

My lover telephoned. She asked me to come and meet her in her office.

It was an October afternoon. There were two steaming mugs of coffee on the desk between us. Behind her was a window and across the road was a park. I could see the trees through that window. It was one of those October days when everything is still. But every now and then a breeze would rifle through the trees and a blanket of leaves would come down and then everything would be still again.

She told me she hadn't been feeling too well, she'd gone for a check-up. Nothing out of the ordinary. And the results had come back that morning. And she was HIV positive.

I knew, as soon as the words registered, I knew without having to take any tests myself, without having to see a doctor or visit a hospital, I knew I was HIV positive myself. I knew. Not in my head or my heart or my soul but literally in the blood that was running through my veins. And when I knew that I said to her, Let's stop pretending, let's stop this charade, let's tell everyone who's involved, everyone who should know. Let's tell them. Let's start living one life instead of these two lives we've been trying to keep together and keep apart.

She just sat there and shook her head. She told me she

needed time to herself, to come to terms with this. She needed room for herself.

She shook her head. She asked me to give her time to deal with this.

I said I would but I knew while I was saying it that in the days and weeks ahead I'd telephone and write, that I wouldn't be able to give what she asked for, what I'd promised. I knew, too, that in asking for time we had come to an end.

It was getting darker by then. I could see people hurrying from the other offices. Hurrying to their cars. Hurrying to get home, to get to the pub, to get to meetings. Just as we had done. I thought how simple it would have been to put on our coats and scarves and walk hand in hand across the park. What a simple, ordinary thing and yet we had never done it in public and wouldn't now.

We both sat there and it got so dark I could no longer see the features of her face, just the outline of her hair against the window. She made no move to go and she didn't ask me to leave and I was grateful for that. I thought, as long as we can stay in this room, in this darkness and quietness, nothing that's happening out there beyond the trees, no sickness that's growing inside us can do us any harm. As long as we can hold on to this time, this darkness, then everything will be all right.

I have no memory whatsoever of leaving her office that evening but I do remember clearly thinking, feeling, that as long as we had this we had everything.

Afterwards there came the anger. I blamed God, you,

medicine, me. I'd get into my car and drive at eighty-five, ninety miles an hour along narrow country roads. I'd drive at ninety miles an hour down narrow roads, around blind bends. Sometimes I'd close my eyes and press the accelerator to the floor. I didn't care who I killed or who killed me. I'd drive flat out with the car windows open and I'd scream and scream and scream.

Fuck you, God, fuck, fuck, fuck, fuck, fuck you for what you've done to me. Did you see me on the street? Did you pick me out of the crowd? Did you say, There's a bastard whose broken every rule in the book, there's someone who needs to be taught a lesson. Did you say, I'll give this bastard a dose he'll never forget, I'll let him die in agony? Did you put the finger on me and say, He's the one? Well, fuck you, God.

And then I blamed you. You could have been the one to say no. You could have been the one to say friendship, nothing more. You could have been the one to point out that we weren't in a position to get involved like that. But blaming you lasted about as long as it takes me to say it. Then I blamed medicine. For days I'd sit in my room and hear all these voices going round and round inside my head. I'd close my eyes and see these faces. I got to know these people, these executives of medical companies. I got to know their faces, their voices, their suits, their haircuts, their monogrammed briefcases. I could see these people sitting around boardroom tables in penthouse offices and I knew they had a cure for the HIV virus. I knew it was sitting there in some formula on that table but all I heard were their voices going on and on. Talking all the time about ballpark figures.

We wait till Europe and America catch up with Asia and Africa, they'd say. That's where the money is. Give it till another eight, say ballpark figure ten, million people are diagnosed positive, then we move. We wait till the straights catch up with the gays, they'd say. Then we can go with this. Wait two, three, ballpark five, years. If we do that, if we time it right, they'd say, laughing, we make enough money not just for ourselves and our kids but for our grandchildren to retire. I'd hear all this, day after day, going round and round inside my head and there was nothing I could do to let it out, no valve that could release the voices and the faces. And I'd think of people like you and me and Simon, depending on these bastards.

And then I blamed myself. I had three or four days free that Christmas and I'd get up early in the morning and go down to the kitchen and clear the table and then I'd lay out all these blank sheets of paper with a calendar in the middle. I became determined to work out when, exactly, I had contracted the virus.

It couldn't have been this week because you were away on a course. It couldn't have been that week because I was on holiday. It couldn't have been this week because we didn't meet. In the end, I narrowed it down to one week. It couldn't have been the Monday because, when we made love, I wore a condom. Same thing on the Tuesday. In the end, I narrowed it down to the Thursday of that week. By then you were on the pill and we were safe.

I remembered that day so clearly in every detail. We made love in my bed in my room that afternoon. While we were making love the front door bell rang. I'd left a note pinned to it saying that I was unavailable until half-past six and anyone who wanted to see me should call back after that time. I knelt up and looked through the net curtains of my bedroom window. I saw a figure scuttling through the gateway and then I turned back to look at you. Your mouth was slightly open and your tongue ran across your bottom lip. Your hair was streaked across your forehead. I bent down and ran my tongue between your breasts. Your skin tasted hot and salty. My tongue continued across your belly and into the wet warmth between your thighs.

Eventually, I got back to blaming God.

One dark afternoon in January I walked into the church, up the aisle on to the altar, up until my face was pressed against the tabernacle door. The church was empty but I don't think it would have mattered then even if it hadn't been. I pressed my face against the metal door and shouted. Why did you do this to me? Why, why, why, why to me? That most pathetic of questions to which there is no answer because there is no valid question in the first place.

And then I tried to pray. I'd get down on my knees beside my bed and close my eyes but nothing would come into my head. Nothing. No words. Nothing. And when I'd open my eyes I'd see you lying there in my bed. In the end, I went back to those childhood rhymes:

Now I lay me down to sleep, I pray the Lord my soul to
keep,
and if I . . . die . . . before I sleep . . .
and if I die . . . and if I die.

When I was growing up in the fifties there was still a
shadow of TB hanging over our village. There was a
family living near us, a Church of Ireland family, the
Somervilles, and they had four daughters, Mary and Anne
and Emma and Kate. Mr Somerville worked as a farm
labourer just outside the village. Three of the girls died of
TB. First Anne and then Mary and then Emma. Kate was
the only one to survive.

I remember, as a child, sometimes we'd drive by their
cottage and their washing would be hanging out and my
mother would refer, disparagingly, to TB sheets.

Once Mr Somerville's name appeared in the local paper
for some minor offence, not having a light on his bicycle
or something like that, and my father read out the report
in the local paper and sniggered and said, That's TB for
you, bad blood will out.

I knew I had to tell my parents about my situation. I
drove over one Sunday for lunch and when we'd finished
the meal we sat in the kitchen drinking coffee and then I
told them. I told them I was very ill and that I wasn't
likely to recover. And then I told them I was HIV positive.
I swear, as soon as that registered with them, I could see
the look on both their faces, I could read their minds like
a book, as soon as it hit them. HIV positive. That must

mean some kind of sexual perversion. I could see both of them reacting in the same way. It wasn't my illness or possible death that was of primary concern. It was this sexual thing. This perversion.

After a time my father turned to me and said, Was it Kate Somerville? Jesus Christ Almighty, I hadn't seen Kate Somerville in what . . . eighteen, twenty years, and this was the best he could do?

Later that afternoon I was standing in our sitting room, looking out across the lawn from the back window. That strange room that smells, paradoxically, of furniture polish and dust, that damp room that is only ever used on Christmas Day and Stephen's Day. The door opened behind me and I knew by the footsteps that my father had come in. I heard the creak of the leather armchair near the fireplace as he sat down. He cleared his throat and I knew he was going to speak. I remained at the window, my back firmly to him.

Do you remember the day after your ordination? he said. Do you remember when we came back here to the village? The pipe band was out to meet us, there were bunting and flags and banners all the way down the street and the footpaths were lined with people. And do you remember the three of us walking down the street after the band, you in the middle and your mother on one side of you and me on the other? And do you remember what I said to you? I said, you're no longer our son, you belong to God now.

His voice faltered a little then but he soon found it

again. This . . . this . . . this thing, he said, this . . . sin has nothing to do with your mother or me, it's between you and God. And you have nothing to do with us.

I wanted, there and then, to remind him of that afternoon, that football match when I was twelve years old, but I didn't.

When all of this happened I could, I suppose, have spoken to some of my confrères. Some of them might have been sympathetic. Some would have pointed out how many commandments I had broken. I had failed to honour God. And my father and mother. I had, I suppose, technically committed adultery. I could have gone to the Bishop. It wasn't that I was afraid of what he might say. There was nothing he or anyone else could say that would come even close to touching me now. He might even have been sympathetic. He might have left me in my parish for four or five months and then quietly shipped me off to some convent as chaplain. The nuns would have welcomed me, prayed for me, nursed me and buried me. But I don't want that.

I've always been conscious of my body, of keeping myself in trim. I can still do my press-ups, push-ups, running on the spot. I still look after myself. But in the last few months I've started watching my body for signs, for sores on my skin, for cuts that won't heal. Watching. I don't want to end up like Simon, not able to do anything for myself. I don't want to end up in a sweaty hospital bed some summer afternoon, lying there when I know I should be out running through the forest. I don't want to lie there knowing the angel of death is loitering outside the door. I want to go out and meet the bastard halfway. More than halfway.

I know how I will kill myself and I know why, and it has just been a question of deciding where.

In the end I chose this church. My church. My altar for the past eleven years. Isn't that what it was all about? Isn't that why I was here every morning at eight o'clock, isn't that what people came for on Sunday? The blood sacrifice? By the time I'm finished here they'll be buying a new carpet for the altar, at the very least. I can see my confrères wading through my blood to get to my body. There'll be no hushing it up. No smuggling me into consecrated ground under false pretences! No humbug from my parents or the Bishop. None of that.

I've written you one last letter my beloved, my lover, my heart in this heartless world. You take the ashes and scatter them wherever you choose.

I know why I'll die and where. And how. I've seen enough of this in the line of duty to work it out. Wouldn't Judas have traded his rope for a Stanley knife. Two quick strokes and you're on your way. Virtually painless. Money back guarantee but there's no going back, thank you.

Step one. The ritual. And the practicalities. Roll up the sleeves. Better still, remove the shirt. A few well chosen words. This is my rejected son, who would have been better off becoming an auctioneer like me, marrying and fucking within the sanctity and safety of the marriage bed.

Jesus Christ! Blood. Blood. Blood. As good as the guarantee.

And this is my beloved son in whom I am disappointed but I will send down my own Son to meet him outside the gates of paradise.

Oh, Christ. Jesus, Jesus, Jesus.

Not that I have any faith in paradise. Not any more. The only thing I have any faith in is that afternoon when we sat in your office and I watched the trees and the leaves and the darkness coming down and I thought if we can just hold on to this we can hold on to everything.

the third epistle

It's over. I know that. Even before it's begun. Intuitively. I slept for ten or fifteen minutes and woke with that cold, unalterable certainty that the whole thing is completely over. Of course, there are moves to be made, words to be muttered with diffidence, embarrassment, but really the whole thing is over.

Let me tell you two stories, to put your mind at rest, to remove any lingering doubts that I have expectations of the situation. First, there's the story of the half-waking dream I've just had. I dreamt I'd walked the length of this train, eight carriages, looking for you, examining the faces, searching for yours. I knew you must be on the train. Somewhere. When I'd reached the end of the last carriage, I turned and walked back, searching the faces of the passengers looking in the other direction. But I knew, even before I'd reached the door of the first carriage, that you weren't on it. And I could hear the whispers racing along behind me, like small waves. They were a mumble but I knew that I had made a fool of myself. I felt the sweat drop from my armpits and trickle down my side. And then the whisper passed and raced ahead of me and my heart was banging and the bleak certainty of the final seat beckoned. A man and his wife sat there. Your parents. Laughing. But before I could speak they disappeared and I was standing on a dune above a beach and the wrecked train was behind me, shunted into the long hard grasses. As far along the beach as I could see. Empty but with a terrifying emptiness. A hopeless absence of people. And then there was the smell. I recognized that smell, or something like it. The dark stink of hopelessness, like damp tea-towels left for a week in an empty house.

I woke suddenly and of course there was no sea, only the whited darkness beyond the lighted window of this blizzarded train. And I knew it was over. With certainty. So relax, the pressure's off. I concede. You can read this in the car, with the engine running, and we'll drive out to the house and have a polite meal, watch TV or something, and tomorrow I'll be on my way back to Dublin, that's all.

Let me give you a laugh, though, before you go any further. Do you remember how I'd latch on to a phrase and use it as a kind of mantra? I did it all the time. A line from a song or a verse from a poem, that kind of thing. I was a fake, you said. I didn't have an original thought when it came to love, you said. Well, I had my mantra ready for this meeting, too. A couple of lines from Lorca. I've been repeating them all afternoon. Nothing fake about these, just something to steady myself while I walked across the platform to meet you.

'Dejare mi boca entre tus piernas, mi alma en fotografias y azucenas.'

That was going to carry me through the first moments of discomfort. Don't ask me, when you've read this, to translate. It was meant to be a mantra of passion. Sometime you'll work it out. Or maybe not. I think you may not bother. But if you do get inquisitive, pick your translator carefully. Don't ask the local nuns!

Maybe all that stuff about the voices whispering like a wave wasn't a dream. Maybe I spoke in my sleep. Perhaps they really are whispering the intimacies of my failure from seat to seat. The observant ones, the ones who've already sussed out that I'm not what I appear to be, may have noticed the change in my face. You can't fall asleep hopefully and wake up despondently and not show it. But that's not your problem. There are no problems any more, just a mistake that's in the process of being rectified.

Here, let me throw you a line – literally. Eliot's one. 'That is not what I meant at all.' Tell me that when you looked at me, when you were particularly kind, that there was nothing more to it than friendship. I'll accept it from you. I'll accept it without mentioning how you were flattered by my compliments. We'll let it go at that because you know, as well as I do, that desperate feeling of walking the carriages. Despondency. Let's just be gentle with each other and get this over as kindly as we can. And, anyway, I promised you another story.

I was on a train, and this was not a dream, London to Holyhead. The end of the summer of 'seventy-five. Coming back from my three months on the building sites, a few quid in my pocket, a few possibilities. Anyway, this guy sat opposite me and then a girl sat beside me. It was a Friday evening, the first weekend in September. The three of us got talking and as soon as he placed my accent the guy started on a string of Paddy stories. He wasn't being funny, just vicious. And he knew exactly how to hit. I had nothing much to say but this girl began to put him in his cage, bit by bit, until she'd edged him out of the conversation altogether, until there was just her and me talking. She was on her way home from work in London, back for the weekend to some small village. All the time she was talking she looked straight at me. I remember she had brown eyes and brown hair cut straight across her forehead. When we reached her station, I helped her with her suitcase. At the carriage door, she opened her carrier bag and handed me a box of chocolates. And then she got off and waved and walked down the platform. I've always thought I should have got off that train, taken a chance on getting off but I let it go.

That's all. No point much. I just wanted you to know that I have never been sure about the gesture, sometimes too little, sometimes too great, sometimes nothing at all.

Tomorrow I'll be back on this train, not writing then. I'll sit with my eyes closed and feel the rhythm as the sun flashes off the melting snow and puddled fields. There will be regret. Of course there will. That I've said too much. But some things say themselves. There is no real choice. You know that, too. It's just that hearing what you don't want to hear is altogether different from saying what you can't help saying!

And don't you feel relief, now that you've reached the end of this? Haven't things fallen back, more or less, into their proper places? Can't you relax a little, not completely, not until I'm safely stowed away, but just a little? I regret the pain, for both of us. And I regret not sleeping in your arms. I should have liked that. Very much. To sleep and wake with you.

I haven't taken things beyond that point, so it's OK. Relax. Relax. It's all back in its proper place. And thine is the kingdom and the power and the glory.

laburnum

The local paper was waiting for me when I got in from
work. I don't mean the freebie rag that passes for a paper
where we live, I mean the local paper from back home.
The real paper. My father sends it every week. Among
other things, it tells me who I should write to to sympa-
thize and who I shouldn't expect to see around the village
when we go back in the summer. I left the paper unopened
until the children were in bed, something to look forward
to. When my wife had gone out to her swimming session I
spread it out on the table in the kitchen and started with
the local notes. When my wife returned, I showed her the
photograph.

'So that's him,' she said.

She had never seen Cooney, though she knew him quite
intimately, from my descriptions. He had been the scourge
of my childhood. Before I was even born he'd fallen out
with my father about some court case or other. My father
had appeared as a character witness for someone Cooney
was prosecuting. After the case Cooney had come up to

our house and, finding my father out, had been abusive to my mother. Insults were traded for a couple of weeks and then both sides settled into life-long silence. And now he had retired as principal in the local school and was pictured at his presentation.

'I expected horns,' my wife said.

'He was too clever for that.'

'Well, at least he won't inflict himself on any more kids. That's something.'

'He should have been fired years ago. The abuse we took from him was unbelievable. I don't know which was worse, being in his class or the fear of going in,' I said. 'I can laugh at most things but there wasn't even black comedy in his case, just plain malice. Can you imagine what it's like, when you're nine, being told by your teacher that you're dog-ignorant and that it's hardly surprising, given your pedigree. It was all insinuation. You were being hurt but you couldn't see the wounds, just feel them.'

'Well, he's gone,' she said. 'No point working yourself up about it.' And she went off to make some tea.

When we'd finished the tea she asked me if there was any other big news. 'No,' I said, flicking through the paper and stopping, again, at the photograph of Cooney and all the village dignatories.

'Don't start again,' she said.

'I just want to see who was there.'

I looked at the faces. Some familiar, some unfamiliar. The parish priest, the new principal, the area inspector, the other teachers, a few parents, the county councillors.

'There's another interesting man,' I said, indicating the local rector.

'Why?'

'He was once my prospective father-in-law.'

'Tell me more.'

'Another time,' I said. 'It was a strange situation. His daughter was a strange girl, very strange.'

'Attractive?'

I nodded.

'But very strange.'

'And she didn't marry you.'

This summer we went back to the village for six weeks. My uncle was in hospital and my father needed help with the farm. The children loved the freedom of the place and my wife was within driving distance of friends in Dublin. There wasn't an awful lot to do, I was there for reassurance. My father, as usual, had things ticking over nicely.

One weekend my wife took the children up to stay with friends in Meath. I was left to my own devices. After tea, on the Saturday, I walked down to the village for the paper. I was late. All the shops were closed. I decided to walk to the end of the village and back across the fields. The place was all but deserted. A few teenagers were lounging on the wall of the rectory and, above them, in the lowest branches of the huge laburnum, three or four others were swinging noisily. The place was obviously unoccupied. It was June, the rector was away on holiday.

I hadn't been in the grounds in almost fifteen years. On an impulse, I decided to go in. The girls sitting on the wall ignored me, the boys in the branches sniggered and carried on with their swinging. The windows were still the same shabby maroon I remembered. Always in need of a coat of paint. Always slightly faded.

Between the garage and the house there were roses. Blue Moon. Above them was the window that had, once, been the light of my life. I peered through the grubby panes. Everything was covered in dust sheets. Perhaps the rector had grown more prosperous. Or less. As I rounded the corner I heard a shout and then another and then a flurry of jumping and running and laughter. I turned to go back and, as I reached the gable, I saw a figure crossing the gravelled yard. It was Cooney. As he walked the delicate flowers from the shaking tree continued to fall about him. I thought they would never stop. The evening was still and they came down straight between us.

He spoke almost immediately. '*Laburnum angroides*.' He pointed with the walking stick he carried. I remembered that tone of his voice immediately.

I said nothing.

'The largest I have ever seen. The fullest flowers and the stoutest trunk I have ever come across in this species. I come here to enjoy it, to savour its strength and beauty and stillness.'

I waited for some cutting comment about the boys who had been playing in its branches but instead, as if to illustrate his disdain, he poked at the fallen petals about his feet. Then he walked the few yards to the house and rested on the sill. I could imagine him doing that every evening.

'It's a different world in here,' he said. 'The quietness. I tried it in my own garden but it isn't the same. There's something about the atmosphere in here. Different from us. I believe it comes from generations of quiet certainty.' He went on poking at the settled yellow flowers. 'But imagine living here and never seeing this tree at its most splendid.' He shook his head.

I stood my ground, waiting for him to finish, certain he had no idea who I was. He wouldn't have seen me in twelve or fourteen years.

He picked a flower from the sill. 'A lot of people mistake this for mimosa but it's not.' He got up slowly and walked towards the gate. I allowed him out of the yard before I followed. I had nothing to say to him. When I reached the gate I saw that he was standing, with his back to me, on the path outside. I pulled the iron bars shut behind me.

Cooney spoke without turning. 'Were you ever in there in your time?'

'Not really,' I said.

'Every summer, for four weeks, I go in. While they're away. It's a holiday in itself. A different world.'

He walked away. I heard young voices sniggering in the graveyard across the street. I pushed the bolt home on the gate. My hand was the colour of rust.

*

We were back in the village at the end of the summer for my uncle's funeral. Someone mentioned that Cooney was failing and, coincidentally, the following evening, as I drove along the River Road, I passed his daughter pushing him in a wheelchair.

A month ago, my father mentioned on the phone that Cooney was dying. He'd been moved to a hospital here in Dublin. I thought of calling to see him. My wife said I should.

'He knew you that evening. He made his move, his gesture. It was more than you expected. You should bury the hatchet at this stage, for God's sake. Just drop in.'

'I'm not sure,' I said. 'I'd have nothing to say.'

'Bring him a book, a gardening book. I'll come with you if you want.'

'I don't think so.'

'Try,' she said. 'You mightn't even get in. Leave the book at least. Let him know.'

'No,' I said, finally. 'He probably doesn't even remember that evening. He may have thought I was someone else. I'd only confuse him. I'd better not.' But, instinctively, I knew he remembered. 'Anyway, Jesus, when I think of what he put me through in school,' I said, frantically searching beyond that summer evening and hearing, again, his words spat at the nine-year-old me. 'No, leave the vindictive bastard as he is, there's no point, I couldn't carry it through. Let him go.'

children

'Does this fella know where he's goin' at all? We were round here before. That's the depot over there and that's the second time we passed it!'

'It seems he's lost all right.'

'I had a feelin' this was goin' to happen.'

'He's pulling in.'

'You run up and tell him, you know the lie of the land.'

'Peter is gone up.'

The young man behind the wheel leaned forward and wiped the condensation from the windscreen of the Morris Minor. His father huddled into his overcoat, ill at ease.

'Are you warm enough, Mary?'

'Fine,' his wife said from the back seat.

A car swung out of the cortège ahead of them and moved off. The hearse followed and then the line of cars.

'Now maybe we'll get out of the bloody park.'

'Peter knows the way.'

'They should've let him lead in the first instance.'

At Castleknock Gates the Morris stopped and father and son got out.

'I'll get a bus back from here,' the young man said. 'You'll have no trouble following them.'

'Right.'

His father sat in the driver's seat, anxious not to lose sight of the fading cars. His mother slipped the young man a ten-shilling note. 'You won't be late for your lecture, will you?'

'Not at all.'

'We'll see you next weekend, then, or the one after.'

'Yes.'

'Take care of yourself.'

'We better be goin',' his father said uneasily.

'You'll explain to Joan why I couldn't go down?' the young man said.

'We will, of course.'

'Goodbye then.'

The car jolted away. The young man smiled and crossed the road to a bus stop.

'I knew they'd get lost. I had that feelin'. It's bad enough drivin' this far on a bitter day without gettin' lost on top of everythin'. God knows, it's enough torment for them without this. They should've put someone that knew the way outta Dublin with the driver. Just because Halpin trained in the depot doesn't mean he remembers his way round the Park. It must be twenty year since he was there.'

162

They were well clear of Dublin, clear of the uncertainty that confused and upset him.

'I was glad Robert came to the hospital. It took a weight off my mind not havin' to drive down the Quays.'

He was almost amiable now where he had been short-tempered all morning. Driving into the city with him had been a penance. She had struggled to keep silent as he lost his way time and again, ignoring her advice and then turning on her for not being of any help. When, eventually, they had reached the mortuary chapel there had been no sign of Robert. When he arrived, halfway through the rosary, she breathed a sigh of relief.

'There's great heat outta that,' he said, tapping the heater. 'You can't beat the Morris for heat. The wind'd go through you outside the chapel.'

'It won't be a pleasant evening for it,' she said.

'Was there any mention of the postmortem?'

'Not that I heard. I didn't like to ask.'

They were silent for a time, the cars keeping a steady pace, trickling through the dry countryside. Outside May-nooth a cyclist dismounted and walked back three steps along the road with the funeral procession.

'There's something I didn't think we'd see this side of the Shannon,' she said.

'It's unusual all right.'

'Is this a good stretch?'

'As far as I know,' he said.

'Will we have a cup of tea then?'

'We might as well, it's a fair steady pace.'

She leaned into the back seat and took a basket from the floor. While she unscrewed the flask top he took in the cars veering to the right at a bend. 'That's a biggish crowd, eight cars. It's a good number to travel this far.'

'Yes,' she said, handing him a plastic cup of tea. 'I'll leave the sandwiches there beside you. Can you manage?'

He nodded. They ate and drank in silence, the clear November afternoon slipping by outside, ditches of leafless alder; shopboys putting up shutters on another half-day; children returning to school. She repacked the basket and put it carefully on the floor.

'I don't know how people drive with a radio in a car,' he said. 'You couldn't concentrate rightly with that goin' all the time. I see them in every second car. I wouldn't be caught with one. Whole dangerous.'

'I suppose.'

Suddenly they were veering right and then left.

'Damn sheeptrack from here to Moate,' he said testily. 'One patch I hate.'

'I remember it.'

'A bloody sheeptrack,' he repeated. 'A twist or turn every twenty yards. He'd want to ease up in the hearse. This is no place to be tryin' to catch up on lost time.'

He bundled himself over the steering wheel, trying to gauge the spasms of the car in front.

'How's Joan bearin' up?'

'She was all right. The cemetery will be the worst part.'

'Yeah.'

'Thanks be to God there's no question of him being left in the church overnight.'

'No, the quicker the better. Danny is in a daze over it.'

'I know the kind of daze,' she said sharply. 'He's no help to her. I said it from the start, she should never have married him. Dada was against it and he was right. It's support she needs now and he won't be capable of giving it.'

'I suppose he's upset too.'

'We all know what has him upset. What use is that to her, I ask you. No use when he's needed.'

He let the matter drop. They drove on through Kilbeggan. A car pulled on to the road behind them.

'That Rita,' he said. 'It's good of her to come this far. She must've taken the day off.'

For a few miles the sun caught the side of the car and it might have been summer as it splayed across the open fields. Then, as quickly as it had come, it was gone and there was a crust of sleet on the glass.

'By God, that'll make a pleasant evenin' of it.'

'It might blow over.'

'I hope so,' he sighed.

Three miles from Athlone the hearse rolled into an open yard between battered petrol pumps and a public house.

'They're supposed to stop in Athlone,' she said. 'At the hotel. That was the arrangement.'

'Maybe they're low on petrol.'

The car in front blocked their view of the hearse. The engine ticked over steadily and fog crept up the windscreen. A figure came along the line of cars, a coat over his head. It was Peter. She rolled down her window.

'More trouble. The hearse is broken down,' he said. 'Tim is giving him a hand to look at it. It shouldn't be too long.' He moved on to the next car.

She rolled the window up. The cold air swirled about them. 'That's a disgrace,' she said sharply. 'A bloody disgrace. That should never happen. Never.'

The sleet turned to rain and then back to sleet. It lodged in a few sheltered places along the ditch, yellowy white. He turned off the engine and they sat staring at the plupping flakes on the misty windscreen. The car in front moved on. He started the engine and wiped the windscreen with the back of his hand.

'They're pullin' into the yard,' he said.

He parked awkwardly, near the pumps. Her brother came across through the sleet.

'How are ye? I missed ye at the mortuary.'

'Are we going to be long here?' she asked crossly.

'Looks like it. The driver is ringing in to Athlone to see if he can get a replacement to take us on to Galway. This one is bunched. Gears.'

'How long will that take?'

'Depends,' her brother said slowly. 'If there's a driver available it could be soon, otherwise it could be an hour. Depends really.'

She sighed.

'If it takes any more than half an hour it'll be pitch dark before we get into Galway,' her brother said.

'I'm going over to see Joan,' she said, opening the door. 'Are you coming?' A woman had come out of the public house, carrying a tray of tea things. 'That's thoughtful of them.'

'Danny went in and ordered it,' her brother said, turning his face away from the sleet and brushing it from his collar.

'Oh, indeed, he would be inside,' she said tartly.

'Will you come in and have a cup of tea,' her husband asked. 'Or something?'

'I have no intention of breaking a funeral journey to go into a pub,' she said. 'And neither I hope have you.'

'Sure there's nothin' else to do,' her husband said. 'We might as well have a drink.'

'Well, don't forget you're driving. I have no desire to be in a car with someone carrying drink.' She sighed loudly. 'I'm staying with Joan. Obviously her husband has as much concern as you two.'

She strode across the sleety gravel and climbed into the car in which her sister sat.

The driver of the replacement hearse waited for the pub to empty before carrying the flimsy white coffin across the yard. Peter collected the three bunches of flowers and laid them on the wooden panelling. They moved off again. The low sun was in their eyes crossing the bridge at Athlone, a halfpenny of the day remaining.

When they were clear of the town she launched her attack, spitting the words ahead of her, not looking at him.

'I might have known you'd be the first into the pub, you and Danny and that brother of mine. Good God, you couldn't keep out of it, could you? Not even out of respect? You couldn't let the chance go by. And then we had to wait for you and the rest of them to come out of the public house before the funeral could leave. Christ, man, have you no self respect? Even if you haven't would you not have consideration for me? Standing there waiting. Or for Joan. It's a funeral we're at, you know, not a football match.'

'I only had one, to keep the cold out.'

'Don't make me laugh,' she said, turning towards him. Her tone was bitter now. 'How did the rest of us keep warm? Why does it always have to be you? The rest of them stayed outside, they knew what was right. They went to the trouble of getting a cup of tea for their wives. I had to ask Peter to do it. There was no question of that crossing your mind of course, not at all.'

'The trouble with you is you're unsociable.'

He knew, as soon as the words were out, that he had been foolish to say anything.

'Unsociable,' she screamed. 'Is this a social occasion? Don't you dare open your mouth to me again or I'll get out of this car and travel with someone else. Don't you speak another word. I've had enough for one day. Enough, do you hear?'

There was silence for a few seconds and then she said, with a finality that cut him, 'He was your godson, you know!'

They were still fifteen miles from the village when darkness fell. Snow was plummeting out of the night. It was well past seven when the cars slowed to a walking pace and the people who had sheltered in ditches and doorways fell in behind the hearse. The sparse lights of Oranmore grew large. He parked the car and they walked with the crowd. Joan walked with the priest, down the crisp path from the cemetery gate. Peter walked with Danny. Ahead of them the undertaker carried the coffin, flanked by two altarboys and an elderly man, picking out the line of coping with bicycle lamps. Those behind stumbled, trying to stay on the path.

They were at the grave before they realized, the small pile of clay lost in the snow. The coffin swung down easily, a timber puppet on two ropes. The first shovels of soil fell between the gravesides and the narrow boards. They plumped into the snow. The torchbeams swayed, avoiding the coffin, resting at people's feet. The curate raised his voice above the gravel on wood, intoning the sorrowful mysteries. Danny wept loudly. Joan looked out over the heads of the crowd about her to the light from the railway signalbox.

*

They left the house shortly after ten. He hadn't touched a drop. He was silent as they drove out of the village. She wondered if her words had bitten too deeply.

'It's not too bad to drive back, is it?' she enquired.

'No,' he said. 'The snow isn't stayin'. It'll be all right.'

'You're not too tired?'

'No.'

Crossing the midlands the sleet turned to rain and he relaxed. He knew these last forty miles like the back of his hand. Tullamore, Geashill, Portarlington, Monasterevin, Athy. The desperation in the curate's voice came back to him, fighting sodden clay and foolish crying. He knew it well. After twelve years it was there as fresh as ever. The Jubilee nurse rushing in and out of the kitchen with basins of water. Mrs Dunne making pot after pot of tea, trying to talk down the screams from the room. Garvey, usually so dapper, coming down soaked in sweat. The horrible silence after hours of pain. The nurse telling him to stay where he was and let her rest and Garvey calling him to the back door and telling him he'd have to bury it himself, they wouldn't allow it in the cemetery. It.

He had crossed the square to Hendersons. Even at that hour there was a light there. Jack knew what to do. He'd been through it twice himself. Mrs Dunne tacked a sheet into a box he'd used for keeping nails and screwdrivers. They were turned out on the floor of the shed. The nurse brought it down wrapped in towels. He put it into the box without looking and brought it over to Hendersons. Jack tapped the nails into the lid and put a white cross on the scored wood.

'We'll stay up,' Jack said. 'It's near three, it'll be light in an hour. We'll go out then.'

They pushed the Prefect to the end of the lane, so as not to waken her, and then made off through the loveliest of August mornings, Jack telling him where to turn. They parked on a straight stretch of road, under crab trees, and he carried the box across three fields, Jack following with a spade.

There was nothing left of the church ruins but mounds of grass, more or less a rectangle, in a tiny, untilled field. They took turns at digging. Pigeons flappered in and out of the trees at the other end of the ditch. The ground was hard and they turned up pieces of granite as they dug deeper. A straying sheepdog made towards them from the road.

'Go on, shoo,' Jack shouted. Pigeons rose and settled again. As they closed the grave he shook holy water on the box.

'It's a thing I can never understand,' Jack said, walking back to the car. 'I'm as good a believer as the next man but I never understood havin' to do this.'

'Are you sleepy?' she asked.

The lights of the town were below them.

'No, no, I'm wide awake.'

'I must have slept for a while.'

'You did.'

'We're nearly home.'

'Ten minutes,' he said. He wanted to lean across and touch her hand but he hadn't done that in years.

the fourth epistle

The snow is gone. Five days and the countryside has rid itself. The odd white rag in sheltered corners but, to all intents and purposes, the snow is gone. What did I expect? That it would last for ever? That anything would last that long? Did I expect I could climb on to a train, travel through snow and step off at the other end into a past untouched? That's exactly what I expected. I travelled in expectation of arriving in the country we once inhabited.

And you were there, waiting on the platform, smiling. I got off the train, bag in one hand, a letter in the other, mumbling Lorca's lines to myself:

'Dejare mi boca entre tus piernas, mi alma en fotografias y azucenas.'

As if a poem had the power it once possessed. I assume the power remains but I have lost the knack of hammering the sparks just as I have lost the power to deliver the expected Sunday messages. But that's another bag of tricks! I travelled hopefully, knowing the lilies remained, oddly appropriate. There were lilies from you at the funeral. Weren't they lilies? I'm sure they were. The conversation in the car was polite. When we arrived, you showed me my room, hoped I'd be warm enough and went away to read my letter. Afterwards, you berated me, gently, reminding me of your nineteen years of marriage and what they meant, of how close you were, of how long ago that was, of how we were different people then. You even sympathized. All around you, on the coffee table, behind the couch, envelopes and letters and your bundles of memoriam cards with the smiling photograph and you're sympathizing with me! But bit by bit the gentleness went out of it. Had I not considered you? Had I no understanding of the rawness you were feeling? Wasn't I abusing our friendship, wasn't I?

Your tears began, welling and flowing, unwiped while you went on talking. And all I could think of was the sincerity of the man who stepped on to the train in Dublin, a man whose head was filled with reasons why the past should not be left in a tea-chest for someone else to dispose of in fifty years time. And the man seemed like a shit. I knew he wasn't but he seemed to be. When the time came to go to my room it was a sweet release. If you'd knocked on my door and asked to sleep with me I'd have left the house in search of lodgings. How could I have so mis-judged my ability to explain? Then, last night, after the politeness of four unquiet days I said I thought it was time to go. You nodded from across the table in the warm pine kitchen. You were God in heaven and I was the little boy with the lame excuses. We finished our meal and the small talk started flowing. I was telling you about my parish plans. You were talking about the land. I felt relief at the thought of getting back to Christmas cards and stale news. Everything I had written to you seemed overblown, pointless, stupid.

And then I couldn't sleep. I opened the curtains and peered into the starry darkness, looking for something familiar in the uncoloured landscape. There was nothing, nothing recognizable, nothing to hold on to and as it got brighter I was terrified by the fact that not one tree or field or gate emerged that I could recognize and remember. I was convinced that I would never find anything that had been there as we grew up. The past was in a heaven locked and barred. To ease the panic, I worked my way back through the previous days, back on to the train out of Dublin. I wracked my brain for something. Something. Anything. The girl who'd sat across from me, who had borrowed my newspaper while we waited for the train to leave. Lying in the sick light I reconstructed her face and voice.

'I can't read once the train starts moving.'

'With me it's buses.'

She smiled and went to find herself a cup of coffee. I stole a glance at her student card. The stern photograph. Her Christian name. I daren't move her purse to read the rest.

Lying in the well of this morning I recited the options. Exodus. Numbers. Deuteronomy. Chronicles. Micah.

They became the mantra to get me to the day. And they did.

So here I am. A man on a train, on a journey through rain. All of this is irrelevant, apart from the fact that I got through and getting through was a greater feat than might be imagined.

What does the man across the table see? A man writing, a book open on the narrow table. I'll tell you what he's reading. It's a poem, a prayer, a plea, a song about a woman. A prophetess is what it says but she was a woman. She took a timbrel in her hand and all the other women went out after her, with timbrels in their hands, dancing. And she called on them to sing. I've begun to sing again. I'll make a timbrel and sing with her. I'll dance with her. I'll put my greeting in this letter and carry it in my jacket pocket until I meet her.

Listen! Do you hear that? The timbrels crashing and the dancers singing and singers shuffling in an uneasy dance. And listen, listen to the silence after they've gone. Only one woman left in the space where they were dancing, only one silent tambourine. Only one voice and then that voice is silent. But it doesn't matter. I'll dance for her. I'll do the talking. Sit here, across from me. It was late but not too late.

I'm on a journey. I'm in a train and I have this letter, waiting, by way of explanation.

street

i

The May sun had shrivelled and blistered the street all day. Now, in the late Saturday afternoon, it was settling into something more bearable. Gerry MacGrath sat in his chair, just inside the door of his chemist's shop. People were coming into town, forsaking the deck chairs in the prematurely colourful gardens, to rush the weekend shopping before six o'clock.

Earlier, the sun had measured him, like an undertaker, but now it was creeping up the courthouse wall, on the far side of the street. The woman from the chip shop came in and nodded to him. She took a packet from the shelves and walked to the counter. One of the girls came, smiling, to serve her. During the morning and mid-afternoon there had scarcely been a dozen customers. The girls had worked away, restocking, their pricing machines clicking like crickets in the heat. Now they were posed behind the counters, their brown faces and white coats pleased him.

Their hair shone, their fingers were spotless. In a way, he was proud of them. Satisfied by their youth and beauty. His mind drifted.

In the storeroom the sun would be patching the walls. He loved the cardboard smell of that room. It was the only thing that remained from the days when he had come to work for his aunt. The only room that smelled the same. Even now a breath of that warm dry room took him back to nineteen-thirty-nine. Now that had been a summer. He had stayed in digs outside the town and every evening he cycled to the cricket club, bat, cap and whites tucked under the carrier of the bike. As soon as tea was over he was upstairs for them and on his way.

'Don't forget a drop for the road,' Mrs Flaherty would shout.

'I won't,' sprinkling his forehead as he crossed the yard.

On Sundays they'd hire two or three cars or cycle if the match was near enough. Afterwards there was tea and a hop in the local hall and then home with songs and ringing bells in the darkness, stopping to grope for a dropped jumper on the road. Shouted goodbyes in the square and up the hill to his digs. Mrs Flaherty would have a tray left on the kitchen table, a teacloth draped over cold meat, bread and butter. Often, the light of day was on the curtains as he got into bed for a three-hour sleep.

He had been at work in the storeroom on the Monday morning after the last match of the season when his aunt had called him into the shop.

'Father Moran wants to see you.'

'Where is he?'

'I put him in the kitchen.'

'Thanks.'

He crossed the hall into the pantry that passed for a kitchen. The priest was sitting on one of the two chairs they used at lunchtime. He was a big man with bushy eyebrows. His umbrella was propped against his knee. It hadn't been opened in five months but it went everywhere with him.

'Sit down, sit down, sit down,' the priest said.

The only occasion on which they had spoken together was when he had put his name down as a church collector, halfway through the summer.

'How are things, how are things?'

'Well, thanks.'

'Good, good,' the priest smiled. 'I'll tell you, I wanted a few words with you. A few words to ourselves.'

'Right.'

'You're a cricketing man, they tell me.'

'Yes.'

'You play a lot.'

'Yes.'

'Good too, good too, I hear. I don't know much about the game. I was more into the running myself, until the weight caught up with me.' He tapped his stomach.

'I'm all right.'

'It's a healthy pastime,' the priest said. 'Good exercise. But there's something I wanted to talk to you about. I

decided I'd wait till the season was over. Make it easier.'
The priest paused, as though Gerry should know what
was coming next. 'Well, anyway,' he continued. 'You
know the club, the cricket club, is not of our, ah, faith.'

'Pardon?'

'It's a Protestant club, Protestant and Methodist.'

'Is it?'

'It is. You're the only Catholic in it.'

'Am I?'

'You are and . . .' The priest breathed a long sigh, his
eyes stayed firmly on the floor '. . . I don't want to stop
anyone enjoying themselves but people are talking, people
are coming to me. I thought, maybe you could take the
winter break as a time to step out.'

'Are you joking, Father?'

'No, no, I'm not, Gerry. I wish I was. It's difficult.'

'No one said anything to me.'

'They wouldn't,' the priest said. 'No, they wouldn't,
would they? You're new here. Anyway, they wouldn't.'

'Do you agree with them?'

The priest laughed a dry laugh.

'We're talking about cricket. A game.'

'But we're not,' the priest said quietly. 'This is a small
town. You're a professional man. I don't know. Maybe
you could organize a team in the parish if the game is that
important.'

His eyes lifted from the floor, there was a look of
hopelessness in them. He shook his head and smiled.
'No,' he said. 'I don't know if you can see this from the

outside. It just seemed a good time. The end of the season and all.'

He lifted his hands and opened them and then let them fall back on to his knees. He sat for a moment and then, suddenly, he stood up and stuck out his right hand.

'I'm glad we had these few words. I'll be on my way. Think about it. Think it out. Good luck to you.'

Back in the shop, his aunt smiled, her glasses perched on the end of her nose. 'It was probably worse for him than you,' she said.

'Wait till he hears we're starting a badminton club for the winter.'

The shop was filling and emptying. A man and woman were examining the prices of dental floss. One of the girls pointed out the extra length of the dearer packet. The prettiest of the girls and the brightest. Had that influenced him in employing her? Partly. That and her name.

It was at badminton practice that he met Sarah. She was the new teacher in the Church of Ireland school where they played at night. She partnered him. They cycled to matches on the murky Saturdays of the last autumn of the thirties. At the end of October his name was dropped from the list of church collectors. About that time, he went one evening to collect Sarah from her digs. He was met by the rector. Unlike Father Moran, Mr Ffrench was young and slim and had a mop of sandy hair that fell constantly over his eyes.

'I'm terribly sorry to ambush you like this,' he said. 'But Sarah and I were discussing you and she suggested I have a word with you.'

'About my fraternization?'

'Oh, gosh, no, not at all,' Mr Ffrench said. 'Well, not directly. Some of my parishioners have expressed disquiet about your membership of the badminton club and some of them have broached the subject of your friendship with Sarah. I find this most embarrassing.'

'Would you suggest I discontinue the pursuit of both?'

'Gosh, no.' Mr Ffrench brushed his hair nervously from his eyes. 'I see no role for me in this situation. I simply wanted you to know that.'

He told the rector about the priest's visit.

'We have similar attitudes, as you can see. Still, I mustn't delay you any longer.'

And that was all he had said.

She invited him to tea one evening in the new year. He brought her a hyacinth. Her landlady, a widow, served them tea and withdrew. Sarah told him about a tinker woman who had called earlier in the afternoon. 'She offered to tell my fortune for a tanner and, when she'd told it, she asked for a piece of paper and she folded it in three. She said if I gave her a bob and waited three hours before I opened the paper I'd see the face of the man I'd marry.'

He laughed.

'Well, I opened it.'

'And?'

'It was blank.'

'She gave herself enough time to escape.'

'Still, she had a lovely face. Her skin was like a hedge rose,' Sarah said.

Outside the traffic had come to a halt. Cars inched forward. People edged between the bumpers. The street was one long summer funeral, he thought. Music came from the open window of a car outside his doorway.

> Love is no game, no plaything,
> Love is nothing to do with fun,
> Love will get you in the end . . .

The car moved on again, a few feet but enough to lose the music.

They went to the pictures, Sarah and he, one Tuesday night. Father Moran was waiting for him when he locked up the shop on the Wednesday evening. He fell in beside him as he wheeled his bike towards the bridge.

'I want to talk to you.'

'Yes?'

'We had a chat a while back.'

'Yes.'

'I tried to give you some advice. You don't seem to have taken it.'

'No.'

'I have a little experience in these matters,' the priest said. 'Sometimes when you're outside a thing people assume you have no right to comment. I appreciate that. But sometimes it's the outsider that has the clearest view. If I didn't believe that, I wouldn't presume to advise you.'

His tone remained unchanged but Gerry caught a look in his eye and recognized it as something other than dictatorial. It might even have been tiredness.

'I hear you're walking out with Miss Ireton.'

'Hardly.'

'You were at the pictures last night.'

'I thought the ditch-beating days were over, Father,' Gerry snapped.

The look in the priest's eye changed.

'Moral welfare stretches beyond the self-asserted rights of the individual. I have a parish to think of – everything doesn't centre on you and your life, other people are influenced by what they see.'

'I wasn't aware that my moral welfare was at stake,' Gerry said.

The priest walked a yard or two ahead of him, stopped and turned dramatically to face him. When he spoke, his tone was derisory.

'You live in a cocoon, laddie. You're young and precocious and impudent and whether you have the courage to face it or not you're giving scandal by your associations. You may want to believe there's no harm in it but there is. I'm disappointed and displeased. I've seen your likes before and let me tell you the crash, when it comes, will be shattering. You'll learn the hard way that life is not simple. Never.'

Gerry drew level with the priest and stopped, looking him straight in the face. 'At the moment,' he said, 'I'm a friend of Miss Ireton's and I intend remaining such. Now, excuse me, please.'

Gerry put his foot on the pedal of the bicycle.

'You live in a community,' the priest said. 'You need the community.'

'Is that a threat, Father?'

'It's a piece of solid advice.'

'I don't like being threatened,' Gerry said, and then he rode away. He was livid with anger. When he got to his digs, having kicked the tops off a hundred flowers along the roadway, he told the Flahertys what had happened.

'Bloody priest-ridden country,' the old man said.

'Ah, don't mind Father Moran,' his wife said. 'He's fond of the sound of his own voice.'

The new cricket season started. He cycled down every evening to work on the pitch, to paint the pavilion, to practise. The old sensations returned – the sweetness of the first cutting of the grass in the outfield; the feel of the bat handle through the gloves; white figures, dim in a distant position, as the last over was bowled. It was like waking from the winter dream to find a warm reality. Two of the old team had left for England and the war, otherwise everything was the same.

One evening, while he was freewheeling down the hill from the digs, whistling into the wind, he saw a flash of darkness on the road, the bike bucked and a terrible piercing scream lodged for three or four seconds in his eardrum. He braked and dragged his foot along the ground, grinding the bike to a halt. And then, glancing at the front wheel, he dropped the machine in horror. A rat had run headlong into the spokes and been cut to pieces on the metal rods. Blood and sodden fur were wrapped around the wires. He broke a stick from the ditch and prodded the flesh from the wheel. He knew he had to do it immediately or his courage would give way to his disgust. The broken bits of body fell almost silently on to the road. He shivered in the hot evening sun.

He was bowled, first over.

During that summer he went to Dublin, with Sarah, a number of times. The priest no longer spoke to him but neither had the wrath of God fallen on him. In August, he bought a diamond ring. He kept it. Waiting. Sometimes, when he was going to meet her, he slipped the ring into his jacket pocket but he never gave it to her. And then, one evening, when they were cycling home from the pictures, she told him she was leaving.

'I'm going back to Dublin, to be nearer home. I've got a place in a school – starting at Hallowe'en.'

There was nothing to say. He imagined he knew her well enough to realize this wasn't meant to force his hand. He realized that it was too late for that or that there never had been a time when Sarah wanted things to be more settled. Whichever, it didn't matter now.

She wrote to him for a few years. They met occasionally. Then she went to England. He had a Christmas card from her but mislaid the address. He heard she was back in Ireland but he made no enquiries. The ring was somewhere in a drawer. And every day now he expected her to walk into his shop. He firmly believed she would. Every day he sat there waiting, alert in the expectation of her arrival.

'All right, Mr MacGrath.' One of the girls touched his shoulder. 'We're just going now. Are you OK?'

'Oh, yes, yes, fine. I didn't realize it had gone six.'

'Can we give you a lift home?'

'No, thanks. I'll enjoy the ramble.'

'All right. We'll see you on Monday.'

'Yes.'

They were gone. He checked the locks on the back door, took the money from the cash-register and walked out into the sun, locking the door behind him. Darkness was still a long way off.

Once, in a restaurant in Dublin, he had seen a woman who looked like Sarah. He had been with friends and had peered cautiously through the expensive gloom. He hadn't been certain, it probably wasn't her, but he made no move to prove things one way or the other. He allowed himself the illusion.

When the cash was in the bank night-safe, he walked slowly, enjoying the warmth. Up across the bridge, out the Dublin road, along the avenue to his house. Mrs O'Neill would have his dinner waiting. He even felt a little hungry. He was amazed at how well his suit still fitted, at how painless the whole thing was, as if death was still years away.

ii

'Single.'

She didn't move. She was staring at her distorted reflection in the canopy of the fryer.

'Single! Single!' Mark shouted.

'Yeah.' She snapped herself away from the image with its crooked nose and twisted mouth and scooped the crispy potatoes into the greaseproof bag. She wrapped them in brown paper and handed them to Mark. Again, she was fascinated by the ugly reflection in the silvery metal. She gripped the lip of the chip bin as the pain shot through her. She stiffened the muscles of her legs to keep from screaming. As the pain peaked she had to hold herself. The cash-register drawer thudded. She looked along the counter. The street door was swinging closed behind a man, she knew him vaguely. He was a road-worker. He'd been repainting the traffic signs for the past few days. He stepped off the path and made his way between the cars.

'You wanna stay 'wake,' Mark said. 'You wanna keep the job you wanna stay 'wake.' He pushed past her into the kitchen.

The pain eased slightly and she moved slowly, testing herself. Under the counter she noticed the neat rows of fish in their icepacks, waiting for the late night rush. She looked at the blue-faced clock above the microwave. Twenty to two. She wondered how she'd survive till night. The pain shot her again. She doubled over, clutching her stomach.

'What's the matter, love?'

May was standing behind her. Big and warm and caring.

'I've a terrible pain in me stomach.'

'Is it very bad?'

'Sometimes. It goes away and comes back.'

'Is it the curse?'

She tried to say 'What?' but the word was sucked out of her by another explosion of pain.

'The curse, is that it?'

'I don't know.'

'Jasus. What age are you?'

'Thirteen.'

'Have you started your periods?'

'No.'

'Are you bleeding?'

'I dunno.'

'Well go and look.'

She moved towards the toilets.

'Have you anything with you for them? 'Course you haven't. Go in and look. I'll run across to the chemist and get you towels.' She slid the till drawer open quietly.

'I've no money with me.'

'Fuck the money, let bollicky pay, he's not overpaying any of us.'

She went through to the toilets. Outside she could hear May shouting.

'I'm running to the chemist, one of youse look after the place.'

'Where's Margaret?' Mark was shouting.

'She's sick. One of youse lazy cunts do it.'

She sat and waited for the pain to ease. The black-red stain on her pants mesmerized her. She began to rock gently, easing the pain with the gentle movement backward and forward. Her body relaxed.

'Are you all right?' May, again.

'I think so.'

'Are you bleeding?'

'A bit.'

'I have towels here. Do you know how you use them?'

'Yeah.'

'You're sure?'

'Yeah.'

'Well, open the door and I'll give them to you, and then take a few aspirin.'

When she got back to the shop May was shovelling chips.

'Take two of them aspirin and then sit down.'

She did as she was told.

'Is this your first period?'

'Yeah.'

'Did you ever talk about them at school?'

'They did but I wasn't in.'

'You know what they are?'

'Sort of. Eileen Moran told me.'

'You'll be OK once you're used to them. But there's more to it nor that. You'll want to be careful. You could get poled very easy now so don't let any of the smart boys go messing with you.'

'I won't.'

'And you don't have to be going all the way either. They'll tell you everything but all they want is to get your knickers off. I wasn't much older nor you when I got caught and it's no way to be. Getting married or shagged out is no way to start your life so keep your distance.'

She shooed the flies from a pile of burgers and took a single cigarette from her pocket.

'I will,' Margaret said. The pain was easing now. A fog of smoke rolled around her face.

'Are you feeling any better?'

'I am, thanks.' The towel felt awkward but reassuring.

'Take it handy for a while.'

Mark came through from the kitchen.

'You OK?'

'Yes.'

'You wanna go home?'

'No, no. I'm OK.'

'All right. It's quiet now. I'm gonna collect some stuff at the house. You wanna drop home, May, and I collect you comin' back?'

'Yeah. I could do with checking your man. Are you sure you're all right, Margaret?'

'I'm grand. Fine.'

'Paul is inside. You need him, call him.' Mark said.

She nodded. When they had gone she sat at the back of the shop, out of the sunshine. The pain was almost gone now. The street was quiet. It was nice sitting there. Her father would be home. She'd seen him coming out of the Arches at lunch-time, red and beery. Her sister would be in from work soon and they'd fight. About clothes, money, anything. The usual. It was quiet here. There was nothing she missed about home.

'Hello, sexy.' Paul was standing behind her. He ran his hand through her hair. His skin smelled of suntan lotion. 'You like a bit?' he asked, running his hand down her neck and across her breasts.

'Fuck off.'

'You feeling hot like me?' His fingers ate into the side of her breast.

She slapped his hand away. 'Leave me alone.' She stood up and walked to the fryer. He followed her, trapping her against the metal rim. She elbowed his stomach but he laughed.

'Why don't you have good time with me, huh?'

Suddenly, she started crying. He backed away. The shop door opened. She ran through the beaded curtain and locked herself in the toilets. When she came back to the shop Paul was still there.

'Bitch,' he said.

'I wasn't feeling good.'

'Screw yourself.'

*

She walked to the street door and opened it. There was little or no traffic now. Mr MacGrath was locking the door of the chemist shop; two women were talking outside Farrelly's; a dog lay on the path, sleeping. Mr MacGrath passed, nodding to her. She remembered the reflection in the fryer canopy, the pimpled face. She felt unclean. Ugly. But there was nothing she could do about herself, everything was beyond her control. This sickness, her skin, her father, her sister's sullen unhappiness. She couldn't change any of them. She was still at the door when May came down the street.

'Feeling any better?'

'Yeah.'

'Mark is delayed. Is Paul inside?'

'I think he's out the back.'

'He wasn't at you?'

'Not really, the same as usual.'

'He used to do that to me, and I old enough to be his mother, but I halted his gallop. He got me one day, up against the fryer. I said nothing and he put his hand on my tits so I up and drove my knee right into his bollocks, full force, drove them up between the cheeks of his arse. That softened his cough.'

'He's afraid of you,' Margaret said. 'I'd get a belt off him if I did that.'

'If he ever lays a finger on you, love, you tell me and I'll wrap his goolies around his neck. Right?'

'Right.'

'Or maybe I'll use them for ashtrays.'

Margaret laughed.

'Except I'm not joking,' May said.

They were drinking tea. The shop was still quiet.

'I was dead serious about not getting yourself in trouble. You're a lovely young one and there'll be lots of fellas after you but you keep yourself to yourself. We all get notions about ourselves. I'm talking from experience. I was through the whole show and I wouldn't wish it on anyone. I'm not trying to stop your sport. Fuckers like Paul are one thing, you can see through them. It's the clever boys and the nice boys to look out for. I'm just saying.'

Margaret smiled and nodded.

The crowds began packing in about twenty-to-twelve. The smell of beer and vomit mixed with the smell of food and cigarettes. Margaret felt better now. Her father hadn't appeared either. Maybe he'd gone straight home. Often he came in and demanded service and then left her to pay for what he'd eaten but tonight there was no sign of him.

'That'll be a good ride in a few years.'

A voice from the doorway.

'I'd take her now.'

Spittled laughter.

A boy came to the top of the queue. She chatted with him. When he left May asked if she was going out with him.

'Not really. He left me home from the club once.'

'Well, the same boyo's brother has at least three kids that I know of in this town. And blood is thicker than water.'

'He was nice to me.'

'Nice is nothing. I'm telling you.'

May went away, to serve a table in the restaurant section, but when she came back she took up where she'd left off.

'Tracy Roche on your own road, ask her how nice your man's brother was till he got her pregnant.' She stopped. 'Here's your father,' she said quietly.

He was at the door, with two other men.

'Thas my young wan,' he said.

The two men who stood behind him smiled at her.

'Grand girl,' one of them said.

Her father smiled. 'Come up with the right offer now and we're talking.'

They laughed loudly. She noticed a stream of dribble from the corner of her father's mouth.

'Will ya come out some night,' one of the men shouted.

She ignored him. The three came and stood at the counter.

'Will ya darlin'?'

'Piss off,' Margaret said.

'Fiery. I like a bit of fire,' the man said.

'Her mother was fiery,' her father said.

May pushed her aside and leaned across the counter.

'Fuck off out of here. Now.'

'Fightin' Tess,' Margaret's father said.

May leaned out across the counter. 'Listen you, get the fuck out before I call the guards.'

'We're waitin' to be served,' one of the men said.

'Not here, fuckface. And you, you think you'd have more respect for your own daughter.'

Mark came from the back of the shop and lifted the counter door. Paul was behind him.

'Right. Outside.' He ushered the three men through the door. 'Don't come back,' he said quietly.

The three sat in a car, just across the street, a red car, for ten minutes, and then drove away.

'You take no notice,' May said.

'It's OK,' Mark said.

The shop closed at half-past-one. She got her coat. May called her to the table where she sat smoking.

'What happened wasn't worth worrying about. You just live your life. Let him fuck his up but not yours. Right?'

Margaret smiled and nodded.

'Have you got the towels?'

'Yeah.'

'I'll see you Monday then.'

The streets were clear and dry after the steam and smell of the chip-shop. She walked slowly, half expecting the boy she'd talked to earlier to reappear from some doorway but he didn't. She cut across by the convent and into her own road. The night was still warm but there was a breeze coming off the river. The kind of night for sleeping with the bedroom window wide open, she thought. And then she saw a car outside her house, a red car, with three men sitting inside.

iii

Lifted by the breeze of the passing cars, another swirl of dust matted the freshly painted pole with brown flecks. Like one of the old-time photographs, Joe thought, leaning back against the wall and feeling the pebble-dash cutting through his thin shirt. He glared through sweaty eyes and cursed. That was the second time he'd finished the white sections on the cylindrical pole of the stop sign and, again, it was ruined. It was almost lunch-time and half the pole remained undone and then there was the sign itself and that took more care and more time. He bent and stirred the white paint with a piece of alder.

''Scuse me,' a woman muttered, pushing past him with a pram. She clicked her tongue. 'Stupid place to leave paint.'

'Shove it up your arse,' Joe said, almost silently. He painted over the dust particles. A fly became entangled in the oily mess. It struggled momentarily. Joe painted over it. It stopped struggling.

'How's she cuttin'?'

Joe turned. The County engineer.

'Game ball.'

The engineer surveyed the pole. 'Don't tell me you didn't start with the sign?'

'I'll do it after the dinner.'

'It'll drip and destroy the pole.'

'No, it won't. I done the rest this way.'

'Well, fair enough. The rest are all right.'

The engineer took a pipe from his jacket pocket, filled and lit it. Joe wondered how he could bear to wear a jacket in the heat.

'It's a hot one.'

'Yeah.'

'Fecking tar rising all over the place. Come the winter there'll be pot-holes you could bury a JCB in, and do you think there'll be money to do them? There will in my hole.'

Joe nodded.

'You're permanent now, aren't you?' the engineer asked.

'I am, yeah.'

'You're all right then. Some of the boys will be getting short shift come the autumn. Cuts right, left and centre.' He drew deeply on his pipe and then looked at his watch. 'Right, well, I'd better go and look for your ganger, see what he's up to.'

'Fair enough.'

'You'll have them all done by the middle of next week?'

'Yeah.'

'Right. I'll see you Friday.'

When the engineer had gone, Joe put the brush back in its oil-can and looked at his own watch. Twenty to one. He took the tin of black paint in his hand and lifted the

brush from it. He felt the sun full on the back of his neck.
As he painted, he forgot the time and became fascinated
by the white and black circles alternating up the pole. He
thought of the tops of tights, groped in sweaty seats of the
late-night cinema. He thought of Tracy Roche and last
weekend. Very few fellows went out with her, now that
she had the baby. They all talked about her but they
wouldn't be seen around the town with her. She might
be picked up at a dance or a marquee and left home but
that was it. He had met her at a marquee last Friday
night. He was drunk, pissed by the time she sat down
beside him, he'd hardly recognized her with the big black
eyes, smudged with make-up and the blonde hair that had
been auburn the week before. Had he been less drunk he
might have tried to talk himself out of her company but
the short leather skirt and the yellow jumper that didn't
quite cover her brown belly kept him happily with her. He
had vague memories of dancing and then sitting in the
back of a Volkswagen while someone drove them home.
The next morning he hadn't known whether to curse
himself for being with her or to regret being too drunk to
do anything.

She'd stopped him in the street the following afternoon
and asked if he'd got home all right. She was wearing the
same yellow jumper. The possibilities of what he'd missed
had been too much and he'd asked her to the late-show on
the Sunday night.

Suddenly, he realized what was happening. Jesus, he
thought, if someone sees me painting this thing with a

hard on they'll take the prick out of me. He put Tracy Roche out of his mind. He'd finished the black section. It was five to one. Time to get back to the yard for a brew, a thick strong brew to peel the thirst from his throat. He put the paint and brushes into the doorway of a shop.

'Are these all right till after dinner, Mrs Flynn?'

'Fine, Joe, fine, fine.' A voice from the shadows.

The rest of the gang were sprawled in the sun, a small fire burning beside the aluminium hut. The Ganger; Stones; Christy Roche; the Granny; Gerry and the Doc.

The Ganger was writing in his notebook. He looked over his glasses at Joe. 'Was the engineer up with you?'

'Yeah. Happy enough.'

'Good.'

Christy Roche and Gerry and the Doc were playing cards. Stones farted loudly. 'A message from the brain to tell me hole there's a goods train on the way,' he said.

'Rotten bastard,' the Doc said.

Gerry looked up from his cards. 'Any good women, today?'

Joe shook his head. 'Nothin' stirrin.'

'Bar yer trousers,' Stones laughed.

'You get that lot done next week, Joe,' the Ganger said. 'The week after, we're moving out to Halter's bridge, the bend is coming off there.' He took a paper from his pocket and opened it at the racing page.

'Halter's bridge would suit you,' the Granny said to Stones.

'Why?'

'Archbold's country, d'you remember?'

'Oh, fuck, yeah.'

'What was that?' Joe asked.

'Archbold, the railway linesman, he was out the line about three weeks ago, past the bridge and he sees some activity goin' on behind the line hut and sneaks up, quiet as a prick, and what does he see? One of Frank Hickey's young ones, Jane, and the Rogan gouger, the bank manager's son, and the two of them at it, starko bollicko, in the field. Driv to the maker's name in her.'

'What did he do?'

'He said the rosary! What the fuck do you think. He saw it through, what any of us would.'

'Jasus,' the Granny said quietly. 'That young one is well stacked. Imagine a dekko at them tits.'

'What is she?' Stones asked. 'Fifteen, sixteen?' He lay back on the hot ground. 'I'd go down on her like the fuckin' *Titanic*.'

'All right,' the Ganger said, lowering his paper. 'Enough.'

For a few minutes there was silence. The card game resumed. Joe thought about what he'd been told.

'I hear you were with Tracy Roche at the marquee the weekend,' the Granny said.

'And at the pictures Sunday night,' Gerry said. 'I seen you goin' in.'

'But did you see him slidin' out?' Stones asked.

The Ganger folded his paper, stood up, spat viciously and walked away. When he was out of earshot Stones laughed. 'Prunetool can't take it. He's gone off now to pull his wire over Jane Hickey and all in vain. The original dry ride.' The other men laughed. Suddenly, Stones turned to Joe. 'Look at the horn your man has. Can we expect another little fucker from Tracy Roche in the new year?'

'Drop it,' the Doc said, and there was silence.

Joe waited for another attack but Stones had lost interest. He wandered to the perimeter fence and watched a woman cycling by.

'Blue pantees,' he said when he came back. 'Blue pantees and a bald beaver, who could ask for anything more?'

The Ganger came back to where they were sitting. 'Have you a ladder?' he asked Joe.

'Yeah.'

'So had your father,' Stones sniggered.

Joe ignored him.

He set about painting the sign when he got back to the street. The traffic had eased and he was working in the shade now. He worked methodically for an hour, forgetting everything except the job. People passed but he paid them no attention. And then he relaxed, the job was all but done. He thought of Tracy Roche.

He remembered waiting for her at the convent wall at

half past nine. She had been ten minues late and when she arrived she'd smelled of beer. 'Just to ease my thirst,' she said. 'Anyway, I'm better crack.' She had squeezed his arm. 'It's a bit early for the pictures, isn't it?' she said.

'What would you like to do?'

'Nothing, if you're going to be this grumpy,' she said. 'There's no one forcing you, y'know?'

'We could get a six-pack, walk down the line.'

They bought a six-pack in the last pub in town and went down the Barrow line. It was getting dark. Joe felt himself relaxing. They walked on past the other couples until they found a deserted patch. They sat in the orange glow of the lights that came from across the river. He drank four bottles of beer.

'Don't get brewer's droop on me,' Tracy said.

He wished he was drunk.

'It's warm,' she said.

'Yeah.'

'D'you swim?'

'A bit.'

'Fancy one now?'

'Too dangerous.'

'I can't swim,' she said. She lay back and pulled him down beside her. He opened her blouse. He felt her hand opening his zip. She was a quicker worker than he was.

Afterwards, they lay in the orange light, an uncertain sky above them. They stayed at the river till almost eleven. As they walked back towards the cinema, it crossed his mind that she might be pregnant. She seemed to sense what he was thinking. 'You needn't worry. Once bitten, twice shy,' she said.

During the film, he worked his hand up her skirt and fumbled with the tops of her tights.

'Randy cunt,' she said.

He buried his face in her neck and said, 'I love you,' although he knew he didn't.

'How's tricks?' It was the Ganger. Joe was confused, startled. He was afraid to look at the sign, afraid he'd messed it up.

'Great. Just finishing.'

'I brought down your money. Knock off when that's done. Too good an evening to be wasting. Leave the next one till Monday. Pick up a girl or something.' He handed Joe his wage-packet.

'Thanks.'

'That's a good job,' the Ganger said.

Joe left the paint, brushes and ladder at the Town Hall and set off for home. He was crossing the railway bridge when he met Stones.

'Jasus, come on, quick,' Stones said. 'This is too good to miss. Our luck is in.'

'What are you on about?'

'I seen Lady Godiva and yer man goin' down the line.'

'Who?'

'Big tits Hickey and Rogan. If I went after them on me own, no one would believe me. Come on.'

Joe hesitated. He wanted to see her but not with Stones.
'They'll know we're following them.'

'Shite, boy, they'll be too busy keeping an eye on his
cock. Come on.'

They hurried across the station yard, past the jaws of
the freight store doors. The line out of the station was
clear. A tractor was humming.

'Are you sure they came this way?'

'Certain. I watched them from the footbridge. They'll
be past the bend. By the time we get there he'll be buried
in her.'

They stumbled along the railway sleepers. Joe noticed
the leer frozen on Stones's face. In the distance they could
see Halter's bridge and, beyond it, the linesman's hut.
They began to run.

'Keep off the line, just in case,' Stones said.

They trotted along the grass path. Sweat ran into Joe's
eyes. In the fields cattle lay watching them. They passed
under the shadow of the bridge and then ran up the
embankment, flattening the poppies and primroses.

'They should be through that gap,' Stones pointed.
'Unless Archbold is a wanker.'

They edged along the back of the hut. In the cornfield,
on the other side of the ditch, they could see two naked
figures. Seeing what he had assumed was a fantasy took
Joe's breath away. He was intrigued by the way the girl's
hair made a halo about her head and on to her shoulders.
He didn't know why but this seemed a world away from
his fuck by the river. This girl's shoulders were young and

205

brown, her legs were firm, her face was tanned. He wanted to stand there and watch her face. Watch her shoulders shuddering. He heard a sigh and turned. Stones' eyes, too, were fixed on the girl. His breath came out in short, stale bursts. He was masturbating on to the grass where they stood.

Joe stumbled down the embankment, back on to the line, not caring whether he was seen or heard. He began running. Running and running and running, back towards the station but the stale sick smell followed. He ran faster, his feet cutting into the flint between the sleepers, running and running. But there was no escape.

absent child

How often have I listened to this song? Hundreds of times, thousands, in the last fifteen years. I've learned and unlearned it again and now, tonight, I've got inside it and it's inside me. Working its way deeper than ever before, getting under my skin and under whatever it is that's under the skin.

Subconsciously, I must have known when I put the album on that there was something there, something that would unlock the agitation I've felt all day, something that would calm the unsettled way I've been since morning. But now that it's out, now that I've listened, now that I've finally heard, I know it goes back further than today. Of course it does. And this morning seems perfectly clear. Everything that happened then is clear, every shadow is clearly outlined. There's only black and white now. Darkness and light. Life and death. And calmness, yes calmness but not peace. Never peace. Never real peace. That's too much to ask for. Peace is something far beyond my expectations, beyond hope.

'Love is like smoke, beyond all repair.
My darling says . . .'

My darling says nothing. Never, ever again.

Lilac in the jug on the table, the child asleep in the room
across the hall, his even breathing coming in the silences
between the songs, the night air through the open window
from the yard outside. And then the words caught me
unaware.

'The bridges break up in the panic of loss.'

That was it. The bridges broke. The walls collapsed. The
dam ruptured and hopelessness flooded me. I stood in the
brightly lit kitchen and wailed but no sound came. My
body was churning, my throat choking but nothing came
to cut out the sound of the words.

'Whither thou goest I will go
And they turn as one and they head for the plain.'

And yet, on the face of it, this morning was so different,
so full of something else. Joy maybe, certainly forgetful-
ness, almost freedom. Almost because there is no such
place. It doesn't exist. Once we've been through these side-
roads there is no freedom from the memory of what we've
seen or what we've done or what's been done to us. Certainly no freedom from things like this. From this thing.

In this morning's joy something snapped. Something
said no. Something propelled me towards this song and

undid all the years of distancing. How easily normality disintegrates. But how bright it was this morning. How hot the sun. How the lilacs swept in waves over the paths in the park. How certain the sycamores. And the red chestnut burning its candles. I swung the child in my arms, the child who is sleeping now, swung him like a little Icarus into the air and he spread his young wings and laughed and shouted, 'Again, again, do it again.' And I did, throwing him into the blue sheet of sky, catching him as he bounced back into my arms. 'Again,' he said. 'Do it again.'

And then I hoisted him into the dark places where the branches hide the secrets of childhood, into the shadows where the trees are. And he laughed in terror and delight. Higher than he had ever been and darker. Where he wanted to be. Where he feared. This child who is not mine was swinging wildly on the end of my arms, propelled where I had been propelled as a child, where I had propelled another child seven years ago. And his laugh was booming through the spaces between the trees. But it didn't strike me then. Maybe it should have done. There was just unease.

Whatever I've done in the past six months, with this child, I did before with that other, absent, child. Something made me uneasy but I couldn't pin it down. I just moved away and we went somewhere else.

> 'And he leans on her neck and he whispers low,
> Whither thou goest I will go.'

a year of our lives

But I can't, can I? I didn't. I didn't go where he went. And now I know what it was that sowed itself in my head this morning, what it was that waited all day for this song to release it.

That dark place in the branches, that sombre place where there is no sun, even in the height of summer. That cold place reminded me of the other cold black opening that I looked into and knew I was losing him. Wasn't that what terrified me, quietly? The unrelenting terror of shadow that will never lessen, the awful darkness that's real and imagined. Perhaps, in there, in the shades of the branches, he was waiting, watching this second betrayal. I didn't follow him into the first black pit and here I was with another child, playing as if nothing had ever happened, playing as if he had never existed. But he did. He does. Somewhere. Is it as close as that, as close as the shadows in the branches of summer trees? Or is it as far as the clammy silent place under six suffocating feet of clay? Or is it in the desperation of realization that some things are beyond cure, some situations are beyond rescue and his was one of them?

'At home on a branch in the highest tree,
A songbird sings out so suddenly.'

What did he carry with him into death, that small boy? Apart from terror? The knowledge that all the protection he saw in me was not enough. Fear. Maybe the knowledge that I wouldn't be there with him, even if I could be and

210

who's to say I couldn't have gone? Who's to say we wouldn't have walked out together on some other side?

How easy it was to lie beside him on that bed, to hold on to him, to kiss his face and his hands. That was all so easy. And how easy to reassure him but he must have known, in one hopeless moment, that he was on his own, that boyhood, childhood, is no protection against being abandoned.

And what else did he take? One slight scar on his arm. The result of a joke that went suddenly wrong.

'Here,' I said, and I dipped the cooling iron against my palm. And then I glanced it against his skin. He was laughing, even as it burned his arm. I clattered it back on to the ironing board, the red welt rising on his skin.

'It's all right,' he said afterwards. 'It's all right, it was an accident.'

How often did I kiss that scar? Hundreds of times? Thousands? Not often enough.

'It's nearly better,' he said a week afterwards and he showed me the slight scar that will never go away.

> 'The bridges break up in the panic of loss
> And there's nothing to follow, there's no where to go.'

Once the grave is closed there is no where to follow. There's no way through the shadows in the trees. But this is not a punishment, this is not your revenge, this isn't even that. It's my doing. And the tears won't come, only the dry retching that speaks of emptiness and promises emptiness. Forgive me, my son. Wait for me.

Wait for this man in the summer kitchen with the lilac closing as night comes on, this man haunted by the breathing of another child, this man who listens for some of the hope that was written into the song but cannot hear it.

'And the crickets are breaking his heart with their song,
As the day caves in . . .'